China Dream

Red Dust
The Noodle Maker
Stick Out Your Tongue
Beijing Coma
The Dark Road

China Dream

A Novel

Ma Jian

Translated from the Chinese by
Flora Drew

Counterpoint
Berkeley, California

CHINA DREAM

This book is a work of fiction.

Library of Congress Cataloging-in-Publication Data
Names: Ma, Jian, 1953– author. | Drew, Flora, translator.
Title: China dream / Ma Jian ; translated from the Chinese by
    Flora Drew.
Description: First Counterpoint hardcover edition. | Berkeley, CA :
    Counterpoint, 2019. | "First published in the United Kingdom by
    Chatto & Windus in 2018."
Identifiers: LCCN 2018057990 | ISBN 9781640092402
Subjects: LCSH: Politicians—China—Fiction. | China—Social
    conditions—Fiction. | Satire, Chinese—Translations into English.
Classification: LCC PL2948.3.J53 C48 2019 | DDC 895.1/352—dc23
LC record available at https://lccn.loc.gov/2018057990

Jacket design by Ai Weiwei
Book design by Integra Software Services Pvt. Ltd, Pondicherry

COUNTERPOINT
2560 Ninth Street, Suite 318
Berkeley, CA 94710
www.counterpointpress.com

Printed in the United States of America
Distributed by Publishers Group West

10 9 8 7 6 5 4 3 2 1

To George Orwell, who foretold it all

Contents

Befuddled by spring dreams

The instant that Ma Daode, director of the newly created China Dream Bureau, wakes from his snooze, he discovers that the adolescent self he has just dreamed about has not disappeared but is standing right in front of him. It is an afternoon in late spring, and he has been dozing in his swivel chair, his shoulders hunched over and his pot belly compressed into large rolls of fat. This is the clearest indication yet that dreamlike episodes from his past, buried deep in his memory, are rising to the surface again.

'What a negative dream – it didn't generate any positive energy at all,' he mumbles grumpily. 'My fault for falling asleep in my chair.' He drank too much at lunch and dozed off at his desk before having a chance to lie down, so his mind is still muddled. The door behind him leads to a private bedroom with an adjoining bathroom – a four-star privilege awarded only to leaders of municipal rank. His office is on the fifth floor.

The scroll hanging beside the door bears a line of poetry: I DREAM OF FLOWERS BLOOMING FROM THE TIP OF MY BRUSH, which was written, or rather composed, by Mayor Chen last month at the China Dream Bureau's official opening. Mayor Chen usually charges huge fees for writing his own poems on scrolls at official gatherings, but on this occasion he agreed to simply recite the line and let Ma Daode transcribe it at a later date. Ma Daode has not achieved the same level of literary fame. Last year, he self-published a thousand copies of his essay collection, *Cautionary Sayings for the Modern World,* five hundred of which are still stacked, unsold, inside the cupboard behind him.

Now that the bottled-up memories of his youth have begun to escape, this Ma Daode who grew up in the Cultural Revolution, this high official charged with promoting the great China Dream that will replace all private dreams, is afraid that his job will become imperilled. His past self and present existence are as antagonistic to one another as fire and water.

At this morning's meeting, he got carried away. 'Our new president, Xi Jinping, has set forth his vision of the future,' he told the assembled twenty-seven members of staff. 'He has conjured up a China Dream of national rejuvenation. It is not the selfish, individualist dream chased by Western countries. It is a dream of the people, a dream of the whole nation, united as one and gathered together into an invincible force. We have been urged to press ahead with indomitable will. Our job, in this Bureau, is to ensure that the China Dream enters the brain of every resident of Ziyang City. It seems clear to me that if the communal China Dream is to fully impregnate the mind, all private remembrances and dreams must first be washed away. And I, Ma Daode, volunteer to wash my brain first. I suggest we start work straight away on developing a neural implant, a tiny microchip, which we could call the China Dream Device. When the prototype is ready, I will insert it into my head, like this, and any dream from my past still lingering there will vanish into thin air ...' At this, he stood up and mimed pushing the microchip into his ear. It is only now, having seen his past self appear before him, that he can sense what trouble his unearthed memories might cause.

HEY MR DIRTY DREAM, HERE'S A RIDDLE POEM FOR YOU, he reads, glancing down at a text from his mistress, Yuyu. 'A SAPLING OPENS ITS EYES. A BOY SLEEPS BENEATH A HOUSE. A HOLE EMERGES IN YOUR CONSCIENCE. THE SUN SETS BEHIND A WOUNDED RABBIT.' CAN YOU WORK OUT WHICH FAMOUS LINE OF POETRY IS HIDDEN INSIDE

3

IT? Resembling a toad peeping out from a pond, Director Ma looks up, his bulging eyes sparkling with excitement. He may not have achieved Mayor Chen's literary renown, but still, he is vice chair of Ziyang's Writers' Association, and has gained a small following from aphorisms which he posts online, so this riddle should not be beyond him. Sure enough, in a matter of seconds he finds the word hidden in the character strokes of each sentence and texts back the answer: HOW THEY REGRET NOT MEETING BEFORE.

His secretary, Hu, a quiet, middle-aged man who is slightly balder than him, walks into the office. 'I've invited the Disabled Association to this afternoon's Party meeting, Director Ma,' he says without expression. 'Anything else you'd like me to do?' Director Ma always chooses to have male secretaries to avoid romantic entanglements with close colleagues, mindful of the maxim that 'rabbits should never nibble the grass close to their burrows'. In his last job as vice chair of the Civility Office, however, Yuyu came for an interview fresh out of Beijing University, and he was so dazzled by her beauty he couldn't resist hiring her as his personal assistant. He is relieved they no longer work in the same office. After his promotion to the China Dream Bureau, his old post was filled by his former classmate, Song Bin. At the beginning of the Cultural Revolution in 1966, he and Song Bin climbed telegraph poles together to scatter political pamphlets onto their school playground, locked their headmaster in his office and seized control of the school's public address system. But a year later, after the initial revolutionary unity dissolved into the factional chaos of the violent struggle, they found themselves on opposing sides and their friendship crumbled. Fortunately, the monkey-faced Song Bin has more mistresses than he can handle, so is unlikely to steal Yuyu from him.

'Invite the head of the Internet Monitoring Unit as well,' Ma Daode tells Hu, returning the phone to his pocket. 'The Bureau will be merging with them soon, so he'll need to be in the loop.' He exhales slowly and senses the alcohol on his breath seep into his hair.

'But he's not a Party member.' Hu joined the municipal government six years ago after a long career as a secondary-school teacher. He is responsible for writing the progress reports that are sent to the Municipal Party Committee twice a day.

'He's submitted his application, though.' As Ma Daode speaks, the adolescent self from his dream resurfaces and sees . . . *Red slogans everywhere. Zealous youths marching in procession, faces tinted red by a sea of red flags. Mother on the corner of her bed, knitting a red jumper, a red armband pinned to her sleeve, looking just like the women who gather in parks in red Tang suits to sing 'red songs' from the Cultural Revolution.* Ma Daode raises his hand, trying to banish these images. 'Make sure you tape the whole meeting, Hu,' he adds. 'I'll be making some important announcements.' He is annoyed that just as he is about to present the new China Dream projects, dreamlike fragments from his past are disturbing his thoughts.

'Yes, I'll record it on my phone,' Hu says impassively. His poker face and quiet reserve would make him an ideal secret agent. Ma Daode always feels uneasy in his presence. He says so little, Ma Daode is always left with the impression that he is hiding something, or that a piece is missing from his character.

The phone in Ma Daode's drawer vibrates. WHEN THE WIND BLOWS, IT'S ME WISHING I WAS WITH YOU; WHEN THUNDER ROARS, IT'S ME CRYING OUT YOUR NAME. He reads the text, switches the phone off and shifts his gaze to the framed family portrait on his desk, which shows him on the left in a white T-shirt, his wife Juan on the right in a red cotton dress, and between them his twelve-year-old daughter Ming who is now twenty and studying at university in England. The text he just received was from Changyan, a young kindergarten teacher who likes to write online fiction.

He rubs his chin and gazes out at the huge new forecourt which is being paved in limestone slabs. Never before has his mind been in such disarray. He wonders whether the 'red song' contest he organised recently is responsible for stirring up his buried memories. He thinks of the photograph of himself as a toddler in a sailor suit standing between his parents. Because his mother was dressed in a traditional cheongsam, his sister was afraid their family would be denounced as bourgeois, so she kept the photograph hidden for years. It was only at Spring Festival this year that she finally dared take it out and email a scanned copy to him.

Last week, he posted two photographs on WeChat. The first one shows him with eleven other teenagers in front of the Buddha Light Temple in Yaobang Village, where they were sent after the violent struggle as part of Chairman Mao's programme to re-educate urban youth through hard labour. He spent his time there as a 'sent-down youth' toiling in the fields and teaching in the village school. The second is a photograph of him wearing an army cap and green fatigues, dancing the male lead in the revolutionary ballet, *The White-Haired Girl*, after he was summoned back to Ziyang four years later to join the county propaganda troupe. Both photographs received many likes, and his mistress Yuyu gave them three grinning emojis.

His eyes drift back to his wife in the family portrait

... Do you remember how, after we joined the troupe, you and I would stroll down Drum Tower Street every evening? What a sight we were! You, skipping gracefully by my side, your long braid dangling to the small of your back. And me: slim-hipped, broad-shouldered, wearing the two-tone Italian brogues my father brought back from the Korean War. There were no other shoes like them in the whole of China. As the young people today would say: we looked cool. I admit, I had a flat arse and walked like a woman – but those were minor faults. Who would have guessed that Young Skinny Ma would become the Old Flabby Ma slumped here today?

Over the years, Ma Daode's eyes have narrowed and his nose and mouth have broadened, but when he opens his eyes wide, his pupils sparkle like glass beads, making him look youthful and full of life. His first and oldest mistress, a woman called Li Wei, likes to push his lids further apart with her fingers and tell him to look her straight in the eye.

WHAT ARE YOU UP TO? ARE YOU IN THE OFFICE? The icon after this message is of a cartoon girl with hennaed hair.

GETTING READY FOR AN IMPORTANT MEETING, Ma Daode types back on his Three Star phone, which has a larger screen than the other two in his drawer.

In reply he receives: I'M FEELING HORNY. COME AND

8

GIVE ME SOME ... followed by a cartoon emoji of a blonde woman with large breasts juddering up and down.

RUB YOURSELF THEN, he types, working out at last that the sender of these texts is an estate agent called Wendi. When she wears her tight, pale grey suit she looks like the prim secretaries in Japanese adult videos. Earlier this month, Ma Daode included her in his list of top twelve mistresses, whom he names the Twelve Golden Hairpins after the beautiful maidens in the Qing Dynasty novel, *Dream of the Red Chamber*.

IF ONLY YOU COULD COME TO MY OFFICE AND KISS ME ... After Director Ma reads this message, he draws a deep breath into his lungs and happily contemplates the evening delights that await him. Tonight he will choose her to be his companion. His other phone buzzes.

GOOD AFTERNOON DIRECTOR MA. THIS JUST APPEARED IN THE COMMENT SECTION OF THE CHINA DREAM WEBSITE: 'IN THE MORNING MEETING, THEY SNORE; AT LUNCH, THEY BELCH; IN THE AFTERNOON, THEY YAWN; DURING OVERTIME, THEY GAMBLE; IN THE EVENING, THEY SLEEP WITH WHORES; AT NIGHT, THEY GO HOME AND BEAT UP THEIR WIVES ...' SEEMS LIKE A DIG AT CORRUPT OFFICIALS. SHOULD I DELETE IT? PLEASE ADVISE.

'A cup of Guanyin tea, Director?' asks his secretary, Hu. 'You'll need to set off shortly.' When Hu removes

his glasses, his eyes look even more glazed and motion-
less. The China Dream Bureau has convened a Party
meeting at two o'clock entitled 'China Dream Goes
Global'. It will be held in the Round Office on the ground
floor, and Mayor Chen and Propaganda Chief Ding will
attend.

'No, get me some coffee,' Director Ma replies. He hates
coffee, but hopes that if he drinks some now, it might
help clear his mind. Besides, he wants to acquire the
taste for it, as his oldest mistress Li Wei and youngest
mistress Changyan are both coffee addicts and often
make fun of his outmoded preference for tea. He first
met Li Wei ten years ago, in a coffee bar she had opened
in the former general post office. After the post office
was demolished, she moved the cafe to the new commer-
cial district, then negotiated a lease to manage the Drum
Tower, a thirty-metre-high building built in the Yuan
Dynasty that recently gained the status of protected
monument. She renovated the red-brick exterior, crenellated stone balcony and glazed roof, and repaired the
vast drum housed at the top which used to be struck at
sunset to announce the end of the day. When the resto-
ration was complete, she opened the tower to the public.
For 10 yuan, visitors can climb the steep wooden stairs
to the balcony, touch the ancient drum and enjoy the
panoramic view of the city. In recognition of her enter-

prising spirit and service to the community, she has been selected to join the Municipal People's Congress.

As Director Ma inhales the steam rising from his coffee, he sees in his mind's eye streets ablaze with red banners and slogans ... *Everything is red – even the paper debris of exploded firecrackers scattered over the ground. For a second, all I saw was a red so deep it was almost black. Clutching a pamphlet announcing that Chairman Mao would greet Red Guards at a mass rally in Beijing's Tiananmen Square the next day, I slung a water bottle over my back and sneaked off to the station hoping to catch the next train to the capital, but my mother ran after me and sent me home. As I walked down Drum Tower Street, I saw elderly men and women smashing rocks against the ground under the steely gaze of teenage Red Guards. Among the sweat-drenched faces caked in dust, I saw my father looking up at me. Then I saw him, head bowed, glance up at me again as I walked past. His face was so filthy it looked as though he had just been dragged out from the earth. Only where the sweat trickled down could I see the colour of his bare skin ...* Although Ma Daode hates being pulled back to the past in this way, some small details that return to him leave an after-taste as bitter-sweet as the five-spiced broad beans he likes to munch before dinner.

Director Ma grabs the document folder from his desk

and follows Hu out of the door. He hears the vast building whir into action: shoes shuffling along marble floors as staff pour in from the streets outside, jostle and collide in the grand lobby and make their way to offices and meeting rooms. He sees his mistress Yuyu walk past. When she clitter-clatters past his office door in her high-heeled shoes, she always leans back to check if he's in, flashes him a flirtatious smile, then swirls round again and disappears.

In the lift down to the lobby, he has to endure Song Bin's tedious chatter. 'You must come and see the rehearsals of our new ballet, *The Qingfeng Dumpling Store*. It's a re-enactment of President Xi's visit to the dumpling eatery in Beijing. Remember – it was in all the papers? He queued up himself, ordered six steamed dumplings and ate them at a communal table. A real man of the people! The store has been packed every day since, with crowds desperate to taste the "Xi dumplings". New branches are opening all over the capital. So the ballet's bound to be a hit. Better than anything your China Dream Bureau will come up with, that's for sure!'

Song Bin still lives round the corner from Ma Daode. When their class of fifteen-year-olds went to help farmers harvest peanuts during the summer half term of 1966, he and Song Bin shared the same bed and blanket. During their two-week absence, Mao launched the Great

empty since June were now filled with the sleeping bodies of students who had travelled from outlying counties to offer support. Baskets of hot dumplings were stacked on the desks, ready for them to eat when they woke up. East is Red members were never given hot meals, and only got to touch one of the two battered Japanese rifles when it was their turn to stand guard. They were no match for the Million Bold Warriors.

Although Ma Daode and Song Bin both survived the Cultural Revolution, they didn't speak to each other again for decades. Last year, however, when the Ziyang Municipal Party Committee and municipal government moved into this new headquarters together, they began to bump into each other and finally said hello. Then at a school reunion, they had a chat over a few beers. Now, Song Bin's wife spends all day playing mah-jong with Ma Daode's wife and, sticking to her like a limpet, even goes with her to the park every evening to practise fan dancing.

When the lift reaches the ground floor, Ma Daode pushes past Song Bin and strides out, his fingers impatiently tapping the mobile phone in his pocket.

The Round Office smells of citrus-scented cleaning fluid. The front half of this massive headquarters is a replica of the White House in Washington, D.C., while the back half is a reproduction of the imperial Gate of

15

Heavenly Peace which stands at the north end of Beijing's Tiananmen Square. It is as though each of the original iconic buildings has been sliced in two and stuck back to back. The White House section accommodates the municipal government and the Gate of Heavenly Peace houses the Municipal Party Committee, but the two are interconnected. Locals have dubbed the building 'White Heaven'. Director Ma has never visited the real White House in America, but has seen photographs online of various presidents seated in the Oval Office, and considers his own office on the fifth floor to be no less impressive. And although, at forty-two square metres, it is ten square metres smaller than Mayor Chen's office on the sixth floor, from the window he can see all the way to the water tower of the Industrial Park near Yaobang Village, where at seventeen he was banished for re-education through labour, and where nine years before that, his family lived for six months after his father was purged from high office.

Propaganda Chief Ding is chairing today's Party meeting. Despite the heat, he is wearing a tightly knotted grey tie like the one President Xi Jinping wore on television recently. He rises to address the eight department leaders seated at the long conference table covered in dark blue cloth, and the two hundred or so Party members in the rows behind. Under his able leadership, incidents of social unrest, including recent protests against forced demolitions, have been spun into positive news stories or suppressed completely, and no bad news from the province has reached the ears of Beijing. With his advanced diploma from the Central Communist Party School, he is destined for promotion to provincial leadership. Mayor Chen, who is seated beside him, used to head the Provincial Party Committee, but was demoted to Ziyang last year by the Beijing authorities after two villagers travelled to the capital to lodge complaints against corrupt local officials. 'China Dream Goes Global' is the most high-profile campaign he has overseen since taking up his new position.

Chief Ding prepares to read out Document Number Nine, issued by the General Office of China's Communist Party, pointing out first that it is a confidential, internal communiqué for Party members only, and that no one should record him or take notes. The document bans from television, print and online media any mention of universal values, civil society, civil rights or judicial independence. 'And freedom of the press, of course,' Chief Ding stresses, discreetly adjusting his black toupee. 'These subversive, Western concepts are used by foreigners to undermine our socialist system. From now on, Document Nine will guide our management of the ideological realm.' His eyes widening with fervour, he adds:

'Tonight, each department must assign staff to eliminate these dangerous ideas from our websites.'

Director Ma thinks how, once his China Dream Device is manufactured, such meetings will become unnecessary: just one click of a button and government directives will be transferred wirelessly into the brains of every Party member in the country. His proposal to set up a China Dream Research Centre in Yaobang Industrial Park to develop the device is lying on his desk. He pulls out his vibrating phone and, shielding the screen with his hand, reads a new message: THE WINE IS POURED, OUR MINDS ARE AT PEACE. IN THE CLOUDS, WE LIVE IN A DRUNKEN HAZE. IF YOU LONG TO TRAVEL, IF YOU YEARN FOR HAPPINESS, DON'T ENVY THE IMMORTALS, ENVY US ... With a pained smirk, he returns the phone to his pocket, then scans the Party members and sees his mistress Yuyu, the captivating author of this message, standing out from the dull ranks of men like a cherry on a cake.

'This is the Chinese Century!' continues Chief Ding, jabbing the document with his finger. 'Before the founding of the People's Republic in 1949, we suffered a hundred years of humiliation: from the burning of the Summer Palace to the Rape of Nanjing we were battered, bullied and slaughtered by foreign imperialists. Then Chairman Mao seized power and proclaimed that the

Chinese people had stood up. Now, after sixty years of Communist rule, the Chinese people have raced ahead. Xi Jinping's dream is that by the 2021 centenary of the Chinese Communist Party, our society will be moderately prosperous, and that by the 2049 centenary of our Republic, our economy will have overtaken America's and China will regain its central place on the world stage. During this crucial, transitional period, the ruling party of China must become the ruling party of humanity. Only then will President Xi Jinping's dream of national resurgence be realised. Only then will his China Dream go global. Only then will the Chinese people be able to go out into the world, take control and achieve the great unification of mankind ...'

'So you want to wage a bloody Third World War now, do you?' Director Ma mumbles. 'Hitler only got as far east as Russia, but you want to take over the globe! Isn't picking fights with little Japan enough for you?' He resents the fact that Chief Ding has risen from a modest university post to such high political rank, and regrets giving him his first government job in the County Propaganda Department he once headed. When Ziyang was promoted from a county town to a municipal city, Ding jumped three ranks in one go to become a major leader of the Municipal Party Committee. Mayor Chen is seated between Ding and Director Ma. He is a plump, affable man with lightly permed hair. His breath smells of tobacco and Coca-Cola. Director Ma likes him. Thanks to connections which he made while securing a Master's in America, Ziyang is now twinned with San Diego.

Chief Ding is still speaking: 'If we meld traditional Chinese values with Marxist ideology, the China Dream will be embraced by every nation. Then the world unity so desired by Genghis Khan will be accomplished by our generation of Party leaders. The United Nations will move their general headquarters to Beijing and we will establish communism throughout the world ...' Realising he has spoken for too long, he takes a sip of water and says: 'Now, let's ask Director Ma to discuss the China Dream projects in more detail.' He leans back into his chair and the cool breeze from the air conditioner wafts up to his shoulders, lifting the hairs at the back of his toupee.

Director Ma smiles at Chief Ding, Mayor Chen, and at the rows of heads behind them, and concedes that coffee is indeed better at clearing the mind than green tea. 'I have sixteen projects here, proposed by various districts of Ziyang,' he begins. 'First, let's discuss the "Golden Anniversary Dream" that Peace District is organising. Fifty elderly couples have already signed up. The grand ceremony will be held at Yaobang Industrial

Park. Foreign businessmen based there are keen to sponsor the event, as long as Mayor Chen cuts the ribbon. I suggest we should aim to get a hundred couples, and schedule the ceremony to coincide with our first of October National Day celebrations. The title will be: "Golden Anniversary Dream, colon, China Dream".'

'Great idea! Other cities have had mass weddings, but I've never heard of a mass golden wedding anniversary celebration before. I'd be happy to cut the ribbon.' Mayor Chen smiles and strokes his phone with his pale, plump hand.

'Stay off the booze this time, or you'll end up snoring again,' quips Chief Ding, nodding in his customary way. A wave of chuckles ripples through the rows of Party members.

'Always teasing me, aren't you?' Mayor Chen smiles. Last week, at the opening ceremony of Yaobang Industrial Park's Garden Square, he drank so much rice wine he fell asleep on the podium while he was waiting to give his speech.

'You really think we can find fifty more couples in this city who have been married for fifty years?' asks Commander Zhao of the Demolition Bureau from his seat in the front row. When the general post office was being torn down, Director Ma begged him to save it, but he wouldn't change his mind.

'There are always lots of old people dancing in the riverside park every evening,' replies Director Ma. 'If we can't find enough there, we can rope some in from neighbouring counties.' In a flash he sees the high perimeter wall of his old secondary school ... *If I climbed to the top and crawled along to the right, I could see the pond in the school's forecourt with the miniature rockery mountain in the centre. When we pushed Teacher Li into the pond during a struggle session, the pink water lilies were stained black by the ink we had poured over her head* ... Afraid that his adolescent self is resurfacing again, Director Ma quickly swallows a sip of water and focuses on the black characters printed on the sheet of paper on his lap.

'What about all the widows and widowers? Won't be much fun for them having to watch all the old couples stroll past hand in hand while their own spouses are lying dead in their graves.' The chair of the Women's Division has a thick rural accent. She used to work as a gynaecologist for the county Family Planning Office, and was awarded the title of Advanced Worker for performing sixty-four abortions in one day.

'Only married couples will be allowed to attend the event,' replies Director Ma. 'We've drawn up measures to keep everyone else away.'

'My parents wouldn't be seen dead holding hands!' the chair of the Women's Division replies. 'They won't even stand next to each other for a photograph. If you forced them to take part, their miserable frowns would definitely turn the event into a negative news story.'

'Yes, just think!' the Trade and Industry Bureau Chief interjects. 'All those decrepit pensioners hobbling onto the stage, hunched over their walking sticks. Some of them will be deaf and blind. Others won't have washed in years. Won't exactly create a mood of optimism, will it?' He shakes his head and looks down at the mobile phone and notebook on his lap. His leather shoes look far too shiny.

'Well, we can invite some silver anniversary couples as well – they won't look so ancient. And we must make sure to bar anyone with extreme views. Some old people these days spout out all kinds of dangerous nonsense.' Zhou Yongkang is the head of the Municipal Political and Legal Affairs Commission, and enters the headquarters through the Gate of Heavenly Peace.

'Don't worry about any of them frowning,' Old Sun calls out from the third row. 'If we give them silk costumes and wads of cash, and promise them a banquet after the photographs have been taken, I'm sure they will smile for us.' Old Sun officially retired from the Civil Air Defence Office six months ago, but he still likes to turn up for work every day and offer useful suggestions at Party meetings.

The chief of the Food and Drug Administration Bureau, who is sitting beside him, says: 'No need for any expensive banquet. Give my parents a bowl of soy milk and a dough stick, and they'll grin from ear to ear!'

'But we must treat our elderly citizens with respect,' says Mayor Chen earnestly. 'Filial piety is the bedrock of Chinese culture. The older the person, the more veneration they deserve.'

In answer to Yuyu's latest text: AM I PRETTY? Director Ma tries to send a smiley face emoji, but taps the wrong icon. She replies: WHY SEND A SAD FACE? YOU WANT ME TO CRY? He looks over to where she's sitting, and among the Party members' heads sees her glossy black hair shimmering like the shell of his mobile phone.

'Having elderly people celebrating the China Dream will add gravitas and a sense of history,' says Chief Ding, loosening his grey tie. 'Now, Director Ma, please move on to the second project.'

Ma Daode clears his throat. 'Well, next on the list is a major new ballet called *The Qingfeng Dumpling Store*, devised jointly by the Civility Office and the Cultural Bureau. As we all know, the section chief of our local brewery is the spitting image of President Xi Jinping, so we're hoping he'll agree to dance the lead role.'

'It will be a great hit!' says Song Bin, his monkey face creasing into a broad grin. 'If we unearth some good local talent and pull out all the stops, who knows, perhaps it might get transferred to the Beijing Opera House!'

Director Ma stares at Song Bin who is sitting directly opposite him. Every wrinkle of his ageing face appears to be crammed with dust ... *Soot-filled lines around Father's twisted mouth. Mother lying next to him, her head nestled in his armpit, eyes shut. With my sleeve, I wiped away the foamy pesticide and scraps of half-digested chicken that were leaking out between their lips. If they were alive today, they would be able to stroll hand in hand to the Golden Anniversary Dream celebration along with all the other elderly couples* ... As Director Ma continues to stare at Song Bin, a bitter taste rises from his stomach *... I don't know how my parents met or why they married. All I have is the information from my father's personal record. Name: Ma Lei. 1922: born in Ping County, Shaanxi Province. 1939: joined the army. 1947: joined the Communist Party. 1949: married Zhu Mei. 1957: appointed County Chief of Ziyang. 1959: committed political error and demoted to post of grain auditor of Yaobang Village. 1960: summoned back to Ziyang to work in the County Financial Affairs Division. 1968: died from illness.*

As well as these sketchy details, Director Ma knows that his father went to a missionary school, and that thanks to the basic English he learned there, when he later served in the Korean War he was able to interrogate American prisoners and make inventories of looted goods, and so gained swift promotion to regiment commander. Ma Daode remembers playing chess with his father in their front garden. That was in the early days of the Cultural Revolution, before his father was targeted for persecution. Trying to interrupt his train of thought, he looks away from the Jade Buddha pendant hanging from Song Bin's neck and says in a semi-daze: 'I agree, Song Bin. Ballet is the perfect medium for promoting the China Dream. Once the Internet Monitoring Unit merges with our China Dream Bureau, the supervision of dreams will become integral to our daily work. We will record, classify and control the dreams of every individual, and begin work on a neural implant, called the China Dream Device, which will replace everyone's private dreams with the collective China Dream. In the meantime, we must strengthen the guidance of online public opinion and social media platforms to ensure correct public responses to issues of the day—'

'No need to go into the details of your Bureau's daily work, Director Ma – just focus on the large-scale projects,' Chief Ding interrupts sternly. 'Now, back to the ballet – the Arts Federation should get fully involved this time, and hire all our best writers and choreographers. Promoting the China Dream through literature and the performing arts is the best way to reach the hearts of the masses.'

Director Ma is furious at himself for going off topic. His heart is beating wildly. He pinches his right hand and focuses his attention on the murmur of the air conditioner at the back of the room.

Chairman Zhang of the Arts Federation rubs his hand over the blue tablecloth and says: 'Yes, we're fully on board, Chief Ding. We've just launched a China Dream Poetry Competition. It's our most ambitious literary project yet. And we're also hoping to add more China Dream content to our website.' Chairman Zhang likes to write poetry in his spare time. He too was sent for re-education in Yaobang during the Cultural Revolution. As they both regretted missing out on a university education, he and Ma Daode took a one-year diploma in the liberal arts a few years ago. Ma Daode remembers how, back in Yaobang, Zhang used to spray 666 Insecticide on the crotch of his trousers to keep mosquitoes away. It smelt so foul no one dared go near him. With alarm he feels memories sprouting in his mind again like mushrooms after the rain. *If my past keeps bursting through like this*, he thinks to himself, *I will fall apart.*

'Promoting dreams through poetry,' Mayor Chen says. 'What an inspired idea!'

The voices reverberate around the circular room. Some of the Party members are leaning back in their chairs, eyes closed; others are staring down at their phones; only a few black eyes are fixed on the leaders at the front. Director Ma scrolls through his contact list, taps on Hu and types: RECORDING THIS? Hu replies: YES. Hu is sitting near the front. The specks of light reflecting on his glasses are flickering like candles.

'Replacing personal dreams with the communal China Dream is our Party's main objective,' Mayor Chen says. As he pauses for breath he hears a soft tapping. 'Is that you sending a text, Commander Zhao? I see you have a new iPhone. Just be careful when you group-send erotic poems – you don't want to end up in South Lake Retirement Home!' The home he is referring to lies in a valley below Wolf Tooth Mountain. A former military air-compressor plant, it now serves as a prison for Party cadres of county level and above who have been sentenced for transgressions of duty. Its grounds feature a golf course and a fishing lake. Years ago, the area was rife with mosquito-borne diseases. It was there that Ma Daode and his classmates spent a summer half term picking peanuts. When they formed the Fear Neither Heaven Nor Earth Combat Team on their return, they fought with other classes over paint, brushes and waxed paper needed for their posters and pamphlets. '... The

China Dream encourages the masses to embrace Socialism with Chinese Characteristics. It is very different from the kind of brainwashing that took place in the Cultural Revolution …' The Mayor's voice has faded into a hum so muffled it sounds as though it is coming from another room. Director Ma looks around, but can see no one speaking. He wonders whether the noise is coming from inside his own head. It has a slight nasal twang now. He watches smartly dressed young secretaries hand out bottles of mineral water. The youngest one, Liu Qi, looks like an air stewardess in her navy tailored suit. When she came to ask him for a job, he gave her one straight away because he used to play cards with her father, Liu Dingguo, when he was re-educated in Yaobang Village.

One mid-autumn festival, Liu Dingguo invited our gang of sent-down youths to have a meal in his parents' mud house. We wanted a snack to eat with our beers, so Liu Dingguo climbed over a wall to see what he could steal from his neighbour. A few seconds later, he came back with a bunch of radishes that had been drying in her yard. He plonked them on the table and said, 'That crafty woman. Said she was too ill to work in the fields, but she's not ill at all! She's sitting in her back room right now eating fried eggs!'

Director Ma receives another message: RAINDROPS ARE THE CLOUDS WEEPING. MY TEXTS ARE ME

YEARNING FOR YOU. Realising he forwarded the very same couplet to his oldest mistress, Li Wei, last week, he resolves to stop stealing love poems from the Internet.

To his irritation, he sees Yuyu eyeing him flirtatiously. *How naive she is,* Director Ma tuts to himself. *These kids in their twenties have no idea about the danger of politics, how one small mistake can end a person's life.* During Ma Daode's last year in Yaobang Village, the police stormed into his classroom and arrested a twelve-year-old pupil of his called Fang. Later he found out that all she had done was scrape a tiny piece of plaster from a Mao statue to use as a setting agent for some bean curd. It suddenly occurs to Ma Daode that when he fits the China Dream Device into his brain, all these memories that keep popping up without warning will be forwarded straight to the Ministry of Supervision. This thought makes him break into a sweat. It has taken years of hard work for him to rise from the General Affairs Bureau to his current high position. He has had to learn the precise tone of voice and turn of phrase to employ at meetings such as this. He wonders whether his distracted rambling just now might be a sign of his impending downfall. He scratches his nose and whispers softly: 'Like a live crab dropped into boiling water, as soon as you turn red hot, your life is over.' He came up with this adage in a seafood restaurant while contemplating the precarious nature of success, and it has become very popular online. He suspects it might perfectly describe his predicament right now.

'These sixteen projects have great potential,' Mayor Chen says, checking his watch. 'Their planning and execution will require the concerted efforts of every department. Now I'd like to invite Zhu Zhen to tell us about the China Dream International Symposium she attended in Shanghai.'

'I went to that symposium, and wrote this report when I got back,' Chief Ding interrupts, picking up the document from the table, clearly furious that the Mayor has taken over the meeting. 'You have each been given a copy, so you should all read it before we go any further. I can tell you that the main conclusion of the symposium was that the China Dream is a declaration of war against the reactionary Western concept of constitutional democracy.'

The air conditioning seems to have stopped working. A stale whiff of cigarette smoke in the air transports Ma Daode back to his days in Yaobang ... *Old Yi, who looked after the cattle shed, used to smoke dried tobacco rolled in scraps of newspaper. His mud house was so small and dark, there was no place for him to pin up a portrait of Mao. But my fellow sent-down youths still accused him of disrespecting the Great Helmsman, and reported him to the county armed forces. The packet of tobacco he left behind after he was taken away turned me into a smoker for life.*

Trying to snap back to the present, Director Ma mutters: 'We must conquer the fortress of dreams, eradicate all past dreams and promote the new national dream. All dreams must comply, all dreams must be thoroughly inspect—'

'You're sleep-talking, Director Ma,' Mayor Chen scowls, nudging him in the ribs.

Director Ma jumps up from his seat and with a look of fierce resolve continues more loudly: 'From now on, every individual, irrespective of rank, must submit their dreams and nightmares to me for examination and approval. If they fail to comply, every dream they have ever had, and every dream they ever will have, will be deemed an illegal dream!' Feeling sweat begin to drip down the side of his face, he falls silent and stares out at the sea of black eyes.

Sharing the same bed, dreaming different dreams

GAZE AT CLOUDS DRIFTING IN THE BREEZE, INHALE THE SCENT OF WILD FLOWERS AND LET YOUR MIND GROW CALM . . . Before he enters his apartment, Director Ma deletes this text he has just received and instantly forgets who sent it to him.

He stands in the living room, jacket draped over his arm, wondering why everything feels so strange. His wife soon tells him. 'Been kicked in the head by a mule, have you? This is the first time in years you've been home before six-thirty!' Juan has tied her hair in a bun and is stringing a heap of beans. On the floor beside her are a pair of red slippers, two enamel basins and the portable stereo she will take to this evening's fan-dance session. After she and Ma Daode returned from settling their daughter into her university digs in England, they dismissed the nanny. They rarely invite guests in case they see the boxes of gifts Ma Daode has received for political favours and report him to the anti-corruption unit. With just the two of them in this large duplex apartment now, the place feels empty, so they tend to confine themselves to the living room that has a four-seater leather sofa and a massive flat-screen television. They have even set up a kettle so they don't need to go to the kitchen to make tea. On the coffee table in the middle of the room is a sour-smelling bag of bream that Juan has just brought back from the market.

Director Ma sinks into the leather sofa and stares at the red goldfish swimming around the glass tank below the television. Its protruding eyes remind him of when his mother stood on a bench, her eyes bulging with terror as teenage Red Guards yelled abuse at her. Feeling his heart grow heavy, he looks instead at the black goldfish and its tail splaying out behind it like a long mane of hair ... *Little Fang's hair was as black as that. She had the best calligraphy of all my pupils in Yaobang, and loved to write political slogans on the blackboard. She was arrested a week after her twelfth birthday. When she returned from detention, she didn't leave her home for three days. On the fourth day, I saw her body floating in the village pond, her long mane of black hair splayed out around her head. The slogan she wrote on the blackboard the day she was arrested is still engraved in my mind:* EVERY CHILD MUST JOIN THE REVOLUTION AND DEVOTE THEIR LIFE TO THE PARTY … Last year, Fang's father, Old Yang, secured a licence to breed goldfish in the village pond. Before the government tried to demolish Yaobang last month, Ma Daode paid him a visit. His wife doesn't speak. In the land reform campaign waged by the Communists during Mao's rise to power, she witnessed peasants expropriate her father's land and beat her mother to death with their bare hands, and she never recovered from the trauma. All she can do is sweep the floor, feed her chickens and make corn grits. Before Fang drowned, she liked to take her mother out for walks along the river.

'When you are happy, know that happiness is fleeting; and when you are sad, know that sadness too will not last.' Ma Daode wants to record on his phone this maxim which has entered his mind, then tells himself: *No, I didn't just invent that. Someone forwarded it to me yesterday.* He feels beads of sweat collect on the palm of his hand and rubs them off on his sleeves.

'So, you lost the plot at today's meeting, I heard,' his wife says, delighting in his misfortune.

'Who told you?' Ma Daode feels his memories shooting up like bamboo, enclosing him on all sides.

'Everyone's watching you. What do you expect if you

35

waste your time trying to control people's dreams instead of getting on with your job? Why are you in that stupid Bureau anyway? The Military Logistics Department is brimming with cash now that it's turned itself into the Housing Office. Even the Earthquake Prevention Bureau leaders are richer than you. Why not just cut your losses and take early retirement? If you stay in that job any longer, you'll end up in jail, like all those human rights lawyers.' When Juan speaks, her mouth always twists to the side.

'They'd never send me to South Lake Retirement Home! No way!' Ma Daode's pot belly creases as he reaches over for the remote control.

On the television, a lawyer tells a local news reporter: 'The municipal government must put an end to the violent land grabs. It has no right to sell the peasants' land to greedy developers ...'

'Well, if the government doesn't sell the land, how will it pay the salaries of all the officials and bureaucrats?' grumbles Ma Daode, turning the volume down.

'You've amassed three properties and are always chasing after women – you deserve to get sent to South Lake,' his wife says, returning from the sweltering kitchen, steam rising from her hair. Ma Daode stares at the sweet-and-sour deep-fried fish she has placed before him on the table. He thinks of the text he deleted before entering the apartment, and remembers now that it was from Yuyu. He is worried that she is plotting something. She came to his office after work this afternoon and commanded him to write an official document professing his love for her, then made him stamp it with his thumbprint and the China Dream Bureau seal. He understands now why Song Bin wears a Jade Buddha pendant engraved with the words CHANGE BAD LUCK INTO GOOD FORTUNE. He too must have encountered similar problems with disgruntled mistresses, and learned to patiently ride out the storms.

Juan reappears with a bowl of fried beans. 'When you were courting me, you always took the fish head and left the rest for me,' she says, sitting down. 'Now, look! You dive straight in with your chopsticks and grab all the white meat for yourself.'

'That's because I'm eating fish now, but back then I was fishing for your affection!' he says, forcing a smile.

'Bet you take the head when you eat fish with your young mistress,' she says, looking down at her plate to avoid his gaze. Since their daughter left, they bicker all the time. Ma Daode usually ends every argument by storming off and staying out all night, which infuriates Juan even more.

'Don't listen to those false rumours being spread about me,' Ma Daode replies, still chomping on his food and trying to sound unruffled. 'If you care how you look in other people's eyes, you will be doomed to die in their mouths.'

'Save your crap aphorisms for your girlfriend,' his wife snorts, helping herself to more fried beans. 'Don't worry, I won't hire a private detective to catch you red-handed. I wasn't jealous when I was young, and I'm even less jealous now. Men – they're all the same. When they're poor, they want a wife; when they get rich, they want a harem. It's all such a waste of time.' Ma Daode suspects that Juan knows about Yuyu, but not the other women.

An allergic rash has broken out on Juan's neck from the seafood she is eating. She and Ma Daode take turns to pick at the fish until only the skull, spine and tail remain.

'Our gang of sent-down youths are planning a reunion next Saturday,' she says. 'You've done the best out of us all, so you should host the dinner.'

'Fine, I'll book a table at Fragrance of a Hundred Flowers,' Ma Daode replies.

'Not another sordid nightclub!' says Juan, the light rash now rising to her face. 'Why do you always have to surround yourself with young women? Do you imagine you're Ximen Qing from *Plum in the Golden Vase*, with six wives and ten concubines?'

'But it's the top restaurant in the city now. You can

sit thirty people in the private rooms, and order whatever you want.' He looks up at the opening credits of *When You Loved Me the Most*, and feels his mood lift as he contemplates all the women who are waiting to see him tonight.

'Oh, yes, I forgot: a box of mooncakes arrived today from the CEO of Ten Thousand Fortunes – I hid it under Ming's bed,' Juan says, then goes upstairs to fetch it.

Ma Daode checks his phone and sees a message from the young kindergarten teacher, Changyan: SEND ME A DIRTY JOKE – QUICK! Immediately, he forwards her the one that the estate agent Wendi sent him this morning: A PEASANT WENT INTO TOWN TO BUY SOME CONDOMS, BUT WHEN HE GOT TO THE PHARMACY, HE FORGOT WHAT THEY WERE CALLED, SO HE SAID, 'MISS, DO YOU HAVE ANY PLASTIC BAGS TO PUT PENISES IN?'

Juan brings the box to the table and opens it. The red satin interior casts a rosy glow over her face. 'Ah, he knows I like mooncakes,' Ma Daode says, his eyes lighting up. 'Let me try one.' He chooses a cake and breaks it in two, and where the filling should be finds instead a small bar of solid gold. 'Damn!' he moans. 'I was just in the mood for a proper mooncake. The ones Wuwei County sent us were revolting – they were filled with tinned meat.'

When Juan opens the lower tier of the box her face

is tinted a deeper red by bundles of 100-yuan notes, each printed with the crimson face of Chairman Mao. 'Must be forty thousand yuan in there,' she quickly calculates. 'Looks like he wants a big favour from you.'

'Yes – he's asked me to get his brother a job in the Industry and Commerce Department. What a hypocrite. Always bangs on about cultivating a Communist spirit and opposing commercialisation, while behind the scenes he's doing corrupt deals with shady businesses.' Ma Daode looks up at the television again and switches channels.

'Wouldn't be surprised if he's promoted to Deputy Mayor next year. He'll be at the East is Red reunion as well, so be careful what you say in front of him.' She stares at the heap of gold ingots beside the broken mooncakes, each one looking to her like a small brick of worry. 'Where shall we hide this? The attic's full. Hey, did I tell you your sister's working for a direct-selling company now, flogging fortune-telling kits and good-luck charms? She keeps pestering me to introduce her to new customers. It's obviously a dodgy pyramid scheme. Why don't you just give her this cash and tell her to leave me alone.'

'Is she mad? The government has labelled fortune-telling a "feudal superstition" and is threatening to ban it. Those good-luck charms are a con. The crooks buy cheap leather bags for a hundred yuan, call them "fortune bags", then sell them for ten times the price. Anyway, good fortune cannot be bought with money or charms: destiny emerges only through struggle.' Ma Daode is pleased with this latest maxim. He picks a bogey from his nostril and flicks it onto the floor.

The doorbell rings. In silent solidarity, Juan swiftly covers the mooncake box with a newspaper and Ma Daode hides it inside the cupboard. Then Juan presses her eye to the peephole. It's Song Bin's wife, Hong.

'Let's get moving – it's seven o'clock already!' Hong says cheerfully, as she steps inside. She's wearing a flamenco-style pleated skirt and red lipstick a shade lighter than the one she wore yesterday. She sits on the sofa and admires her long, purple-lacquered nails. Ma Daode taps the vibrating phone in his pocket and watches Juan disappear upstairs again.

'Is Song Bin home yet?' he asks Hong.

'No, he's always back late, just like you,' Hong replies, still gazing at her nails. 'The Civility Office staff seem to get more work than anyone. He keeps having to stay late into the night for emergency meetings.'

'Turn on the television, if you like – Juan won't be long,' Ma Daode says, then rushes to the bathroom to check his texts.

WHAT ARE YOU DOING, MR DIRTY DREAM?

Ma Daode rolls his toad-like eyes and types:

PREPARING FOR TOMORROW'S MEETING. AND YOU? He finds the heated Japanese toilet they recently installed very comfortable to sit on.

ONLINE SHOPPING. JUST BOUGHT MYSELF A PAIR OF ITALIAN SANDALS. EVERYONE AT WHITE HEAVEN WAS TALKING ABOUT YOU THIS AFTERNOON.

IT WAS YOUR FAULT FOR DISTRACTING ME. WHAT WERE YOU THINKING, TEXTING ME DURING A MEETING? NO POLITICAL NOUS. As he recalls his crazed rant at today's Party meeting, he feels short of breath, as though someone is stuffing his chest with straw.

HEY, YOU CAN'T TELL ME OFF – YOU'RE NOT MY BOSS ANY MORE. TOMORROW WE MUST COME CLEAN ABOUT OUR RELATIONSHIP.

DON'T BE SILLY. I'LL COME TO YOU TOMORROW NIGHT, AND BRING A BOTTLE OF VINTAGE XIJIU.

SO YOU'RE BUSY WITH ANOTHER WOMAN TONIGHT, ARE YOU? I'M JUST MISTRESS NUMBER THREE, OR NUMBER FOUR, AREN'T I? WELL, I TELL YOU, DIRECTOR MA, I'VE HAD ENOUGH! TOMORROW I'M GOING TO HAND OVER YOUR SIGNED DECLARATION OF LOVE TO THE DISCIPLINE INSPECTION COMMISSION, THEN WE'LL SEE WHAT GLORIOUS FUTURE YOUR CHINA DREAM HAS IN STORE FOR US!

STOP THIS MAD TALK! YOU'RE UPSETTING ME. Ma Daode is starting to panic.

I WANT TO FLY TO THE NETHERWORLD AND DRINK A CUP OF OLD LADY DREAM'S BROTH OF AMNESIA ON THE BRIDGE OF HELPLESSNESS.

YOU'RE LOSING YOUR MIND! DON'T BE ANGRY WITH ME, I BEG YOU. The thought that she might be contemplating suicide makes Ma Daode break into a sweat.

SINCE I STARTED MY JOB AT WHITE HEAVEN, I HAVEN'T HAD ONE DAY OF PEACE. I WANT TO SPEAK TO YOUR WIFE AND TELL HER EVERYTHING.

MY BLOOD PRESSURE'S RISING, DARLING. I MUST TAKE MY MEDICINE. SPEAK LATER. A chill runs up his spine as he clutches his warm phone. 'Mistress', 'lover', 'concubine' – these are words often heard during the trials of corrupt officials. If any of his mistresses report him to the authorities, he will lose his job and privileges, and return to square one. He usually handles situations like this with ease, but the disturbing memories that have intruded into his thoughts recently have left him so confused that even this small problem seems insurmountable. As soon as he hears his wife and Hong shut the front door behind them, he creeps out of the bathroom and returns to the sofa.

Another text beeps. WHAT'S GOING ON? WHY HAVEN'T YOU CALLED? He stares at the small icon of his oldest mistress, Li Wei, next to this message, and realises he hasn't seen her for almost a month. Over the

43

last two weeks, he has slept with Wendi and Changyan on alternate nights and, despite his better judgement, has met up with Yuyu twice. He decides that he should summon all of his girlfriends to a meeting and lay down some new ground rules. He wonders which woman he should sleep with tonight. Li Wei is at the bottom of his list. No, Yuyu should be – she is about to report him. Maybe he should take Yuyu with him to Li Wei's apartment. That really would be a 'night of blissful debauchery', as the ancients would say ...

We didn't have enough cash to buy my parents a coffin, so my sister pawned a picture frame and a copper wash bowl. She considered pawning my father's two-toned brogues as well, which he seldom wore but always kept polished, but decided to give them to me. With the 30 yuan she raised, we bought a cheap plywood coffin. Now that I'm rich, I could house my parents' bones in a stone tomb, if only I could find them. After we buried the coffin in the wild grove near Yaobang Village, so many Red Guards were buried there as well that it was impossible to know which grave belonged to whom. For those who survived, that wild grove has become a place of nightmares.

'*The swan flies away, never to return / I think back to the past, and my heart feels hollow,*' Ma Daode recites to himself as he pulls on his socks. *Why am I being haunted by all these flashbacks, all these dreamlike visions of death and violence?* The past and the present keep colliding in his mind. Last night, he dreamed of a place he has never seen before. It was a hospital corridor. Both walls were painted green on the lower half and a line of white ants was crawling along the dark crimson floor. At the end of the corridor was a room where the China Dream Bureau documents were stored. He opened the door and saw himself, sitting head bowed in front of a screen, typing the Bureau's annual report, his body shrouded in furry white mould. He could hear children playing basketball outside, and could smell the stench of rot wafting from his decaying double. Then, suddenly, he saw a boy with a slashed cheek, staring straight at him, blood spewing from his mouth. Wendi pinched his nose, trying to wake him up, and whispered, 'What did you say? Whose death do you want to avenge?'

Ma Daode glances at the leftover fish bones and charred beans lying on the table, and remembers the canteen of Yaobang Village School. It wasn't a real canteen – just a small room with a stove in the mud house of a villager who had been killed in the crossfire during a battle on the river front. Two hundred East is Red recruits were sent to that battle, armed with just four hand grenades each. Only thirty returned alive.

Before he steps out of the front door, Ma Daode looks

into the hallway mirror, presses an imaginary gun to his head, and says to himself: 'Hurry up and make the China Dream Device so that all these bloody nightmares can be erased.'

Dreams evaporate, wealth trickles away

Director Ma looks out through the car window at the fields he ploughed when he was a sent-down youth. The blazing August sun has scorched a line of young saplings planted along the Fenshui River. Beyond them, he sees the imposing red-brick warehouse that was built in the 1920s beside a pier where junks from the cities upstream would pick up cargo on their way to Ziyang. Now the river is too shallow for large vessels to navigate, but back during the violent struggle, it was filled with boats and the sound of gunfire. Rival factions fought for control of the river front to ensure the flow of supplies to their forces in Ziyang. It was here that East is Red and the Million Bold Warriors waged their bloodiest battles.

In a battle in May 1968, an East is Red unit from the electricity plant joined forces with a platoon of lower-middle-class peasants and students from Red Flag Secondary School to regain control of the wharf. They approached in rowing boats, firing shrapnel at the red warehouse, and moored at the pier. A dozen workers jumped ashore and charged at the warehouse with machine guns, yelling, 'Enemy forces must surrender or die!' But the Million Bold Warriors were prepared. They tossed hand grenades at the pier, setting it alight. Then they gunned down any East is Red worker who jumped into the river and sent motorboats out to block their escape routes.

Four days later, our unit drove to the red warehouse in army tanks to launch a revenge attack. When we arrived, we saw a hundred black and swollen corpses still trapped beneath the pier ... As Ma Daode stares at the red warehouse now, he catches a scent of rotting flesh *... We held a funeral service for them. One girl stepped onto a stone bench and recited her poem through a mega-phone: "'I'm dying, mother. / Tell the Million Bold Warriors that no crime against humanity will evade the punishment of history.'" We had lit hundreds of incense sticks to try to mask the stench, but it was so overpowering that after reading only two lines the girl stopped and retched.*

On the other side of the river he can see Yaobang Industrial Park. The wild grove has been felled recently to make way for a road that will extend to a steel bridge currently under construction. Eventually the park will spread across the river, doubling in size and engulfing the whole of Yaobang. The villagers have mounted fierce protests against the development, so work has been placed on hold for the last six months. But the authorities have decided that Yaobang must be demolished today, and as Ma Daode lived here in the Cultural Revolution, Mayor Chen has sent him to persuade the villagers to peacefully evacuate their homes.

In a meeting convened by the Demolition Bureau last night, Director Ma heard that the government has offered Yaobang more compensation than any other village that has been demolished in the county. But because of Yaobang's proximity to Ziyang, its farmers have become rich over the last decade selling mushrooms, herbs and poultry to the city, and have built three-storey houses which they insist are worth much more than the compensation offered by the government. Endless disputes have ensued. Director Ma has no choice now but to grit his teeth and make a final, last-ditch effort to bring them round.

He remembers how, a year after he left the village, he returned with his propaganda troupe to perform the final scene of *The White-Haired Girl*. He danced the proletarian hero while Juan danced his fiancée, the white-

49

haired peasant girl. After rescuing her from her mountain cave and overthrowing the evil landlord, he led her off towards a glorious Communist future, leaping and pirouetting across the stage with such dazzling grace that the entire audience gasped in awe. In the evening, Secretary Meng, the village head, invited him and Juan back for dinner. He served them wine and fried vegetables, and even killed a chicken in their honour. The villagers felt proud that the sent-down youths they had looked after for so long had achieved such success.

The straight concrete road along which Ma Daode is being chauffeured in a Japanese Land Cruiser was built in 1978, at the start of the reform era. The riverside track it replaced used to get very muddy after the rain. When Ma Daode first arrived here with the eleven other teenagers from Ziyang, he slipped down into the mud so many times that, in the end, he pulled off his canvas shoes and trudged the rest of the way to the village barefoot, all the while staring at the bottom of the girl in front of him, who would later become his wife. That first evening, Secretary Meng presented each of the sent-down youths a hand-carved whetstone. Four years later, when he received the official letter summoning him back to Ziyang, Ma Daode walked to the end of the pier, took the whetstone from his bag and hurled it into the river as far as he could.

In the distance he glimpses the Cultural Revolution slogan ENEMY FORCES MUST SURRENDER OR DIE painted on a wall which, a second later, he sees is the new perimeter of the Industrial Park. As the car speeds on, he realises that it is he who is daubing the past onto the present.

As soon as the girl on the stone bench retched, everyone else began to vomit as well. Then five ragged Million Bold Warriors were dragged from the red warehouse out onto the pier, kicked in the back of their knees and forced to kneel. Raising a Mauser pistol high in the air, a mad-eyed boy called Tan Dan announced that East is Red had lost one hundred and twenty comrades and that their deaths must be avenged. Then he went over to the five captives and, one by one, shot them in the head and kicked them into the river. After he walked away, all that remained on the pier was half a skull dripping with fresh blood.

Director Ma tells his driver, Mr Tai, to pull up on the side of the road, then he jumps out, clasps his hands together and draws deep breaths, trying to empty his mind. He doesn't want these nightmare visions to distract him from this morning's task. The demolition workers who tried to bulldoze the village last month were attacked so violently that several were taken to hospital and almost died. At noon today, a task force including police officers, armed police and ambulance men will enter the village to enforce the evacuation. On the road ahead, Director Ma sees red flags fluttering from the flat roof of a fake house constructed of concrete blocks and plywood.

'Please get back in the car, Director Ma,' says his secretary, Hu. 'You have a lunch meeting at one with the Prosperity Hotel general manager to discuss sponsorship of the Golden Anniversary Dream, so we don't want to run late.'

'Do we have to go any further?' Mr Tai says nervously. 'What if the villagers drag us out of the car?' He's wearing a smart Western suit and has a long, skinny neck. A young man from the Demolition Bureau is sitting in the passenger seat beside him.

'Drive on, don't be afraid,' says Director Ma. 'I was a sent-down youth here in the Cultural Revolution, so they will treat us with respect.' He then phones Commander Zhao, head of the Demolition Bureau, and Director Jia, head of Public Security, who are travelling in the car behind, and says, 'We'll go in first. You stay here. I'll call if we need you.'

The Land Cruiser pulls up outside the concrete house festooned with red flags. Before Director Ma set off this morning, he was told by his network of informers that this fake house was the protest headquarters, and that the surrounding makeshift watchtowers were equipped only with bricks, metal rods and petrol cans, and could be easily overcome. The fake house stands right at the entrance to the village. There are three toppled telegraph poles blocking the road ahead, and red flags and banners jutting from the trees on either side. The surrounding fields are dotted with other fake dwellings farmers have built in the last few months, hoping to pass them off as real houses and so earn more compensation. These tall shacks have neither stairs nor electricity, and are used mainly for housing pigs and growing mushrooms. Although many villagers have factory jobs in the cities, few have dared leave Yaobang recently in case their land is seized in their absence. To protect their property, they have formed a Land Defence League and take turns manning the various watchtowers. Although they drove back the demolition team last time, it was not a complete victory. Twenty villagers were arrested and thirty were hospitalised; the mushrooms in Gao Wenshe's shack were tossed onto the fields, and a bulldozer dumped earth into the village pond, killing Old Yang's goldfish. Ma Daode has been informed that in preparation for today's assault, Old Yang's son, Genzai, has built a cannon and converted his delivery van into a crude armoured tank.

A group of villagers wanders up, saying: 'No cars allowed into the village.'

'Tell Secretary Meng to come and speak to us,'

Director Ma shouts, climbing out of the Land Cruiser. Above the doorway of the concrete house is a banner that says LAND DEFENCE LEAGUE WATCHTOWER. He peers through an unglazed window and sees villagers sitting at tables playing mah-jong. During the last month, Secretary Meng has phoned him countless times, begging him to persuade the authorities to save Yaobang. Director Ma did pass on his letter of appeal, but he suspects the developers gave Mayor Chen a huge bribe, because the demolition team are under strict orders today to flatten the entire village. Director Ma feels his courage waver. His heart is thumping wildly.

'Secretary Meng's ill, he's at home in bed,' a young man with a shaven head calls out from the back of the room.

'Let me speak to Genzai then, the commander of the Land Defence League,' Director Ma replies, sticking his head further inside the window.

'I am Genzai,' the young man says, walking over to him. 'Wait a minute – are you Old Ma? How come you've got so fat?' Genzai looks as tall as his father, Old Yang, but his eyebrows and forehead remind Director Ma of Genzai's drowned sister, Fang.

'Ah, Genzai, it's you!' Director Ma says, softening his tone, hoping to ingratiate himself. 'Your dear father, Old Yang, was like a father to me. He's well, I hope?'

'Dad told me that since you've become a municipal leader, you've forgotten about your old friends in Yaobang.' Genzai strolls out of the fake house and puts a cigarette in his mouth.

'"When you drink a cup of water, never forget who drew it from the well," as the saying goes. Yaobang Village is still very close to my heart, I assure you.' Director Ma hopes that if he wins Genzai over, the rest of the village will follow.

'Well, tell your friends from the Demolition Bureau to fuck off, then,' Genzai snaps back. 'Unless they accept our demands, we won't let them into the village.'

When Ma Daode first arrived in Yaobang as a sent-down youth, he stayed in Old Yang's home for a few months until the new village school was built. It was a small brick house partitioned by mud walls into three rooms. The central room had only a stove, a few farm tools and some wicker baskets, so Old Yang sectioned off a corner of it for him with a bamboo blind. Fang, who was about eight at the time, would often kneel in front of the stove and put water on to boil. Genzai was born shortly after Ma Daode moved in. Today, in his grey shirt and nylon trousers, he looks like a township clerk.

On the old phone Ma Daode reserves for conversations with his mistress Li Wei, he receives a text from her, saying: EVERY MORNING I WILL SERVE YOU BREAD, MILK AND BOILED EGGS. WITH ME BY YOUR SIDE, ALL YOUR WORRIES WILL BE GONE ... He wishes he could turn this phone off and not have to read her messages, but as he lent his other phone to Commander Zhao, he needs to keep it switched on.

'The expanded Industrial Park will be a boon for you all,' Director Ma says with a big smile. 'You'll be given apartments in the new village just two kilometres away, and well-paid factory jobs. Look at the bridge that's being built. It's been designed by foreign engineers, and will be the first steel bridge to span the Fenshui River. It will make a splendid entrance for visitors to Ziyang.'

'You have some gall, Director Ma! Yaobang villagers looked after you for four years, but now that you're an official, instead of repaying your debt to us, you come and tear down our homes! Ungrateful bastard!' Ma Daode recognises this man. His father was branded a 'former rich peasant' during the Cultural Revolution. He visited their home once. The whitewashed walls, spotless brick floor and earthen teapot evoked the simpler lives of times long past.

Director Ma considers launching into the speech that has been brewing in his mind, but doesn't want to waste it on such a small audience. He turns to the friendliest-looking man, the elderly postman, and says: 'Can you

ask all the villagers to come out? I have some important things to say.'

'If anyone dares destroy my ancestral home, I'll fight them to the death,' shouts a young man in a red baseball cap, standing behind Genzai. 'The twenty villagers who were arrested last time were supposed to be released today, but there's still no sign of them.' Ma Daode knows that this man is an informer. The authorities have promised him that if today's demolition goes according to plan, he'll be given the job of chauffeur to the manager of the Industrial Park.

Director Ma's old friend Dingguo walks up, a big bandage around his head, and shouts: 'We don't need you to mediate!' In the last clash with the demolition team, Dingguo got struck on the head by a truncheon while trying to stop them from arresting his son. Director Ma knows he needs to get him on side as well. Although Dingguo is four years his junior, his hair is already completely white. Ma Daode remembers how Dingguo liked to tag along with him when he went out for walks and tell him the provenance of every dog in the village.

'It's good to see you, Brother Dingguo. Let's try to reach a compromise.' Ma Daode wants to start off by reminding him that he gave his daughter, Liu Qi, her job in the municipal government.

'There's no point talking to you corrupt officials,' says

the informer in the red baseball cap. 'You don't understand: if we can't farm our land, our tractors and ploughs will turn to rust.'

'You feast on exotic delicacies now, Ma Daode,' Dingguo says, 'but we're just lowly peasants. If you seize our land, we'll have nothing left. And how do you expect us to buy a house in the new village with the measly compensation you're offering us?' Although Dingguo has deep wrinkles and white hair, when his face scrunches up with anger, he still looks like a child.

'What about all the wads of cash you have stashed under your bed – why not give a few of them to us?' says a man called Liu Youcai. His grandfather built the red warehouse. After the Communists seized power, his parents donated it to the state and moved into the north-facing outhouse which is warm in the winter and cool in the summer. He is a shrewd little man with a ruddy complexion and dark, hypnotic eyes. As soon as the Daoist temple was built on Wolf Tooth Mountain, he secured a licence to run a fortune-telling stall outside the entrance, and from his earnings has bought himself a Volkswagen estate and a two-storey house with solar panels. Villagers often seek him out for advice and guidance, and before anyone leaves to find work in the city, they always ask him to choose an auspicious date for the journey.

Liu Youcai casts his eyes over the assembled crowd,

waiting for it to fall silent, then turns to Director Ma and says: 'We've been notified that the village will be torn down at noon. No one died last time the demolition team tried to evict us. But if the bulldozers roll up here again, we'll fight to the bitter end. They've sent you here first to sweet-talk us into leaving, haven't they? If you win this battle, you'll be made Municipal Party Secretary, no doubt. If you lose, you'll still keep your job. But if we lose, we'll become rootless vagrants, and will spend the rest of our lives in and out of jail, vainly petitioning for redress. What might we gain from this deal? At most, some menial factory job in the Industrial Park. But just think what we would lose: the ancient Buddhist temple, the historic Liu Clan Ancestral Hall, the unique black-brick courtyard houses, the thousand-year-old locust tree. Our Liu ancestors chose this site for the village because of its auspicious location, with the mountain range stretching like a protective dragon to the north and the life-giving river to the south. In the last two centuries, the village has produced four eminent scholars and three county-level officials. We have resolved to defend Yaobang to the death, not just to safeguard our own livelihoods, but more importantly, to preserve our heritage and our ancestral graves. So, I'm sorry, Director Ma, but we won't be taking your miserable compensation fee.'

'Don't cling to your petty clanship dreams!' Director

Ma replies. 'Embrace the China Dream, then the Global Dream, and the world will be our oyster. You could emigrate to Europe and live in any castle or country estate you want.'

'Think you can fool us with that crap?' Genzai shouts. 'Why don't *you* bugger off to Europe, and visit your old friend Karl Marx while you're at it. We know our rights. Remember that speech President Xi Jinping gave last week? See, we've painted a quote from it on that wall: ANY OFFICIAL WHO CARRIES OUT VIOLENT LAND REQUISITIONS WHICH HARM THE INTERESTS OF THE PEASANTS WILL BE HELD TO ACCOUNT.'

'We've heard Ziyang and Zigong have dispatched a hundred armed officers and eighty riot police here today. But we're not afraid. We have the support of President Xi Jinping himself!' This man shouting from the roof of the fake house is Guan Dalin, the sales manager of the Industrial Park's concrete factory. He can finish a bottle of rice wine at one sitting, and is the only man in the village to have succeeded in marrying a woman with an urban residency permit.

Director Ma feels suffocated and out of place, like a swan trapped in a hen house. In his entire career, he has never faced such hostile defiance.

'We've prepared for this battle,' says Genzai. 'We painted a huge portrait of President Xi yesterday. It's on the roof up there. When we unfurl it over the house, let's see if the bulldozers dare come near us. Did you know that President Xi spent seven years in this province as a rusticated youth?'

'He was sent to the north of the province – he has no connections with anyone down here,' Director Ma replies. 'Have you heard about the violent struggle phase of the early Cultural Revolution, before the Red Guards were disbanded and expelled to the countryside? Back then, even death was no escape from the horror. That red ware-house over there was crammed with bodies. Green-bottle flies were drawn by the stench and clung to the bricks in such big swarms that the whole building turned dark emerald. There were corpses strewn everywhere. Fellow compatriots, I saw it all with my own eyes. I saw two kids from opposing factions both yell "Long Live Chairman Mao" before shooting each other in the head. We mustn't repeat the tragedies of the past. More than three hundred Red Guards and rebel workers lie buried in the wild grove over there.' Sensing that he is sinking into the past again, Director Ma stops talking and closes his mouth.

'The "culture rebellion", or whatever you call it – we know nothing about that,' says the young mushroom farmer, Gao Wenshe, his buck teeth glinting in the sun. 'All we know is that this is our village, and if anyone tries to kick us out, we'll fight to our last breath.'

Director Ma turns to a young man with a pierced nose, dressed in black jeans and a black shirt, and asks: 'What's your name? I haven't seen you before.'

'Don't ask – I'm not from around here,' he replies, waving his mobile phone dismissively.

'His mother, Juduo, has been a great help to us,' Genzai says. 'She moved to Zigong a few years ago to teach in the secondary school. Since the government sent us the compulsory eviction order, she's come back many times to educate us about land requisition laws.'

'Juduo's your mum?' Director Ma says to the young man in the most genial tone he can muster. 'I knew her well. She likes to sing revolutionary operas, doesn't she? I remember at the mass meeting held to condemn *Heroes of the Marsh* as a bourgeois novel, she sang that beautiful line: "I have more uncles than I can count, with hearts that are loyal and red".'

'How dare you talk to me about my mother, you fat pig,' the young man snarls with contempt. 'We've got buckets of manure here ready to feed you and the other swine you've brought along.' The crowd bursts into laughter. Ma Daode wants to laugh as well, but when he thinks that in less than two hours all of these people will be arrested, injured or beaten to death his jaws clench with fear.

'Juduo is one of the twenty people who were arrested

last time and are still locked up in jail,' says Liu Youcai, his dark eyes no longer sparkling.

The crowd continues to swell. Director Ma's phone keeps vibrating, but he's afraid to answer it. He has no idea what to do next. At noon, the mobile phone signals will be blocked. He knows he has been dispatched here purely for show, so the government can claim it was willing to negotiate. But whether he persuades the villagers to evacuate or not, Yaobang will still be demolished.

He lights a cigarette, sucks deeply and looks over to Wolf Tooth Mountain and the field that stretches to the dark woods at its foot. *One evening, after ten hours of hard labour, our gang of sent-down youths gathered at the end of that field to pledge our undying allegiance to Chairman Mao. Juan was trembling with exhaustion, and inadvertently dropped her copy of the* Little Red Book. *Knowing her life would be in danger if anyone noticed her let this sacred collection of Mao's thoughts fall into the mud, I quickly scooped it up and returned it to her. Fortunately, there were so many red flags and buckets about, no one noticed. That night, she came to my bed, told me she had left a glove in the field and asked to borrow my torch. I went out with her to help her find it, and to thank me for saving her life earlier that day, she led me into the dark woods.*

The command to MAKE THE CHINA DREAM COME

TRUE AND FIGHT TO THE BITTER END TO DEFEND OUR
HOMELAND on the red banner hung across the road is
very familiar to Director Ma, as this is what he and his
staff are urged to accomplish when they turn up for work
every day.

The fierce sun has reduced the earth to a fine powder
that shrouds the road. Whenever a motorbike passes, a
cloud of yellow dust lifts into the air. Director Ma
decides the time has come to give his speech. There
must be a hundred villagers here now. A small group
has wandered over to the Land Cruiser to gawp at its
luxurious interior and chat to the man from the
Demolition Bureau. Director Ma climbs onto the roof
of a crushed car, raises a loudspeaker Hu has handed
him and says: 'Fellow countrymen, my name is Ma
Daode. I spent four years here in the Cultural Revolution,
working in the fields and teaching in the village school.
And before that, during the Great Famine, I lived here
with my parents for six months. I cherish these moun-
tains and rivers as much as you do, and I applaud your
determination to protect them. I haven't come here today
to force you to evacuate – that's not my job. No, I have
come simply to warn you that the demolition team will
arrive at noon. If you resist, you will have to suffer the
consequences: destitution, homelessness, even death.
But if you leave peacefully and accept voluntary reset-

tlement, there will be a hundred jobs made available for you in the expanded Industrial Park. It will be the China Dream of National Rejuvenation in action! Fellow countrymen—'

'Stop trying to swindle us!' shouts Dingguo, enraged by the treachery of his old friend. 'The village was promised seventy million yuan compensation, but we've only received nine hundred thousand. That works out less than a thousand yuan per person. If you take our land, how do you expect us farmers to earn a living? In the first phase of the Industrial Park's expansion, forty villagers were given jobs, but half of them have been sacked already. This second phase will be just another empty promise.'

'What right do you have to slap land acquisition notices on our ancestral homes?' an old woman in the middle of the crowd shouts, waving her walking stick in the air.

'Well, half of you signed the voluntary resettlement contract,' Director Ma replies. He knows that the village was built by the venerable Liu family when it moved down from Shanxi Province. The Liu Clan Ancestral Hall has a Song Dynasty stone plaque engraved with the poem: ON THE ANCIENT ROAD, WE BID FAREWELL TO THE LAND OF PAGODA TREES. / A THOUSAND LI DOWN-RIVER, THE WOODS ARE IMBUED WITH FEELING. /

BELOW THE RAIN-DRENCHED WOLF TOOTH MOUN-
TAIN, WE SET UP HOME.

'But if you forcefully evict us today, everyone who signed will lose their right to compensation,' complains a young man. 'What a stitch-up!'

'The government's been colluding for years with crooked developers,' says a woman holding a bag of shopping. 'Look where it's got us! The Fenshui River has turned the colour of black tea – it's filled with dead fish. When we irrigate our fields with it, all the seedlings die.'

Director Ma feels his throat tighten. 'New green guide-lines forced us to close the concrete factory – that's why those workers were laid off. But the second phase will focus on hi-tech, so the new jobs will be secure. If you want a better life, you have to let go of some things. We'll pay you a fair price for your land, but don't expect any money for the fake houses you've cobbled together on those fields.'

'Those shacks in Yiniao didn't have windows but the government still paid compensation for them,' the sales manager Guan Dalin shouts down from the roof.

'Your new village will be built over there, at the foot of Wolf Tooth Mountain,' Director Ma says, pointing into the distance. 'The plans have been approved. In just two years' time, you'll be able to go to your jobs in the

Industrial Park, then travel home on a bus, enjoy a hot shower and watch television in your brand-new apartments. You'll be living the China Dream!' Director Ma is gesticulating so passionately, he almost loses balance.

'Dream-talking again! We could never afford one of those flash apartments with the pittance you're offering us. I warn you, if you don't stop harassing us, I'll get on a bus and set fire to myself like that guy did the other day.' Guan Dalin is referring to a farmer from a neighbouring village who committed self-immolation on a crowded public bus to protest against the seizure of his land.

'Tell the demolition team I've brought a bucket of diesel, and if they dare enter my house, I'll set fire to myself as well.' This middle-aged man dressed in an army camouflage uniform has a pair of binoculars around his neck and is holding a Labrador on a lead.

'That man got bashed in the head last time,' the informer whispers to Director Ma, removing his red baseball cap and wiping the sweat from his brow. 'The car you're standing on belongs to him.'

A group of men walk out from the concrete house, singing: '"This is our native land. Every grain of its soil belongs to us. If an enemy tries to seize it, we will fight them to the death ..."' Everyone knows these Cultural

Revolution songs now that they are played on the radio again all the time. Ma Daode remembers singing this same song, standing on the high balcony of the Drum Tower in Ziyang, waving an East is Red flag. His scalp was sweating then as much as it is now. 'Listen to me, fellow countrymen,' he shouts. 'Two units of armed police equipped with live ammunition will storm the village today, with urban-management officers and assistants. You'll stand no chance against them. "An arm can never defeat a leg", as the saying goes. Surrender now, and trust that the government has your best interests at heart.'

'Enough of that shit!' says Dingguo, grabbing a spade. 'Nothing you say will change our minds. We're ready to die for our village. We've pledged that if anyone is killed today, the rest of us will take care of the children they leave behind. You're lucky you have ties to this place, or we would've beaten you up. So just bugger off now, and tell your bosses we will never surrender.'

Ma Daode knows from Liu Qi that Dingguo's brother was also arrested during the last assault. He takes a gulp from the bottle of water Hu passes him, and says: 'The Buddha Light Temple and Ancestral Hall won't be touched – I promise. Only the cemetery and the old houses will be torn down. Then we'll move the village over there, and you can start your lives anew. Fellow countrymen, seize this opportunity! To those who

68

abandon doubt, new paths will open; to those who relinquish cares, eternal spring awaits!'

'See this kitchen knife?' says a young woman with a huge cold sore as she steps out from the concrete house. 'If Commander Zhao dares to come near me, I'll hack off his dick!'

From the roof, Genzai shouts: 'And what will you do with it when you take it home?' Everyone sniggers, and the dogs start barking as well.

Ma Daode remembers dragging Secretary Meng to the village square for a denunciation meeting. A fellow sent-down youth put a spittoon on Meng's head and the villagers roared with laughter. He can see the same grins plastered on the faces surrounding him now. He tries to return to the present, but his memories are like footballs on a pond: the harder he pushes them down, the higher they bounce up again. 'Fellow compatriots!' he yells at the top of his voice. 'To safeguard the achievements of the revolution, your garrison must be dismantled. Anyone who opposes Chairman Mao's revolutionary line will be eliminated.'

Suddenly he remembers standing outside the Million Bold Warriors headquarters in the last days of the violent struggle. The facade was daubed with Mao's favourite quote from *Dream of the Red Chamber*: ONLY HE WHO IS NOT AFRAID OF DEATH BY A THOUSAND CUTS CAN

DARE UNHORSE THE EMPEROR, which he himself had painted there the previous year. On the hemp-sack barricade before him lay the three hundred bullets his faction had just surrendered. His heart filled with the anguish of defeat. During his first month in Yaobang, where he was sent a few weeks later, it felt so strange for him to sleep without a weapon in his hand that he would often wake in the middle of the night in a panic and be unable to doze off again.

'What do you mean, "Chairman Mao's line"?' Liu Youcai says with disdain. 'This is President Xi's empire now!'

'Yes, sorry, I mean President Xi's China Dream will bring joy to the entire nation!' Unsure whether he is using words from the right era, Director Ma jumps off the crushed car in a fluster and hands the loudspeaker to Hu. Then he checks his phone and sees there are only ten minutes left before midday. Already in the distance he can hear the rumble of advancing trucks and bulldozers. The noise evokes a memory of a Million Bold Warriors platoon marching down Victory Road, rifles aloft, rounding up everyone in sight: boys handing out leaflets, passers-by, class enemies digging ditches in the ground, and herding them into the public square below the Drum Tower, while another unit stood on the roof of the general post office, pointing their guns down at the crowd.

From the high balcony of the Drum Tower the commander of the Million Bold Warriors shouted: 'You dared attack us, you East is Red bastards? If you don't surrender now, we'll round up the whole lot of you.' He was wearing a heavy army coat with a pistol thrust in the belt. As he was the only Red Guard in Ziyang to have attended one of Mao's mass rallies in Beijing, and his father was an army general, he was the obvious choice for leader.

Cross-eyed Chun was standing next to me in the square. He held up a pamphlet and yelled, 'You conservative Red Guard enemies, East is Red will never surrender. We will defend Chairman Mao's revolutionary line to the death!' A second later, two loud gunshots rang out, his knees buckled and he toppled to the ground. Inside my pocket, I was still clutching the pack of cards he'd just given me that was missing a King of Clubs. He looked up at me and said: 'Am I going to die?' 'I don't know,' I answered. 'I'm going to become a corpse, I can feel it,' he mumbled, his voice growing faint. 'Don't bury me in the earth. Don't ...' He tried to keep blinking his eyes, until he opened them one last time and could not close them again.

To break his train of thought, Director Ma looks over to the Buddha Light Temple. It is an ancient grey-brick building with a tall yellow-tiled roof. A hundred years ago, it housed the embalmed corpse of a Liu ancestor who achieved the status of Bodhisattva.

As the bulldozers draw close, the earth shakes and the villagers scatter. The young men climb to the roof of the concrete house, while the women and children retreat to find shelter in the lanes.

Director Ma's phone vibrates. READ THIS ONE, MY AGED SWEETHEART: MAN SEES AN ADVERT THAT SAYS 'NO NEED TO GO UNDER THE KNIFE. FOR A LONGER, THICKER PENIS, SEND US A CHEQUE ASAP.' SO HE SENDS ONE OFF. A FEW DAYS LATER HE RECEIVES A PARCEL, OPENS IT, AND FINDS ... A MAGNIFYING GLASS!! Before Director Ma has time to smile, he hears Liu Youcai yell at him: 'If Ma Lei could see you betraying us like this, he would turn in his grave!' As Director Ma hurriedly deletes the text, he sees his father's face twisted into a morbid grimace. He remembers how he always wore a black quilted jacket in the winter and a long white robe in the summer. After he was condemned as a Rightist in 1959 for blaming the collective farming system of Mao's Great Leap Forward for the famine ravaging most of China, he was removed from the post of Ziyang County Chief and sent to Yaobang to audit the production and distribution of grain. Instead of buckling under, he continued to criticise the system, and wrote an article revealing that Yaobang's annual yields of maize had halved since its farms were collectivised. The villagers admired his honesty and bravery, so although they had been ordered to persecute him, they left him in peace. Eight years later, when Ma Daode was due to be sent to the countryside for re-education, he was able to use his father's connections to secure a position in Yaobang. As it is the closest village to Ziyang, every Red Guard in the city hoped to be exiled there.

The roar of the approaching bulldozers makes Ma Daode judder. Behind them he sees truck after truck of armed police and urban-management officers advance in clouds of dust.

'Let's get out of here, Hu,' he says. 'I tried to help them, but kindness is never rewarded.' Hu dashes out in front and beckons their driver. As the Land Cruiser turns round, Ma Daode sees, reflected on the windscreen, the gruesome blood-spewing face that has haunted his dreams. *The day after Cross-eyed Chun was shot on the square below the Drum Tower, we drove a steel-plated truck into the general post office. I stood on the truck's open back and hurled hand grenades and lances at the Red Guards on the roof.*

Director Ma looks over to the bridge being built across the Fenshui River and thinks of the bodies buried on the other bank, where the wild grove used to be. *One morning we had three boys from the Million Bold Warriors* tied up at the back of the truck, beside the bodies of our six dead comrades. The tallest was a big bully I knew from primary school. Our East is Red anthem was blaring through the loudspeakers: 'They thrust a blood-soaked knife into our throat and assume that we are dead. But we will never die! The East is Red flag will wave on for ever in the sour wind and crimson rain ...' The boy who wrote the lyrics to this song had died in battle the previous week. At the wild grove, we untied our three captives and forced them to dig a grave for the bodies, then we buried them alive inside it. No – that's not exactly true. Before we shovelled the earth back into the pit, we stabbed two of the captives first. We were going to stab the big bully as well, but were afraid he would shout 'Long Live Chairman Mao' as the knife entered his chest, so we stuffed his mouth with twigs and buried him alive with the eight corpses.

IF YOU WERE A TEAR IN MY EYE, I WOULD NEVER CRY AGAIN, IN CASE I MIGHT LOSE YOU ... Director Ma ignores this latest text, and on the phone he is holding in his other hand types: MAYOR CHEN, DESPITE MY BEST EFFORTS TO PERSUADE THEM, THE VILLAGERS REFUSE TO EVACUATE. As he sends it, he notices the signal is fading, so quickly texts the estate agent, Wendi: I'LL VISIT YOU TONIGHT AND FUCK YOU TO DEATH, followed by a line of scowling emojis.

A brick crashes onto the roof of the Land Cruiser. At least it didn't break the windscreen.

From beyond a mud wall a makeshift cannon fires chicken bones and condoms filled with cement powder. The armed police raise their plastic shields to protect themselves, then lower them again. Young urban-management thugs in black T-shirts lift their wooden batons and gleefully lash out at the crowd. Director Ma is now trapped between two police vans and an ambulance.

He looks up at the flat roof of the concrete house and sees Genzai unfurl a huge portrait of President Xi Jinping. 'That's as big as the poster you've commissioned for the Golden Anniversary Dream,' Hu remarks. 'Must have cost them a fortune to laminate.' When he joined the East is Red suicide squad to attack the general post office, Director Ma's comrades took one look at the words LONG LIVE CHAIRMAN MAO on the huge banner hung over the entrance and froze. *I too was afraid to touch that sacred red slogan, but I told them that if we didn't attack we would be killed. So we crawled beneath the banner on our stomachs. As soon as we came out the other side, one of our squad was bludgeoned with a brick and died on the spot.*

'Don't attack the concrete house yet,' Ma Daode calls out to the men in the bulldozers. 'Let's bring Xi Jinping down first.' He is relieved to discover that the thoughts in his head now correspond with the words leaving his mouth. An odour of decay that seems to come from both the past and the present flows down into his lungs. The sales manager Guan Dalin is standing next to Genzai on the flat roof, waving the national flag. Some young men who've returned from factory jobs in the cities have climbed onto the barricades at the entrance to the village and are filming the scene on their mobile phones.

'Remember, our goal is to evacuate the village without bloodshed,' shouts the head of the urban-management team. 'We must move fast this time, and not repeat the mistakes we made in Xiaozhai Village last week.' The fashionable Mohican haircut he gave himself this morning doesn't match his official uniform. His team have donned yellow safety helmets and their black Alsatians are barking at the village dogs. Although the battle has not yet started, Director Ma sees broken chair legs caught in branches and the streets of Ziyang strewn with bricks and dead bodies after another attack on the Million Bold Warriors. *We carried our dead comrades to the riverbank, washed the blood from our hands, changed into clean uniforms and held a memorial for them below the Drum Tower. Corpses of our enemies lay all around us. In the hot June sun, they swelled and let off a foul stench. One dead girl had flies all over her face and an ice-lolly wrapper stuck to her hair. After today's*

clash, there will be no corpses left on the road. There are
ambulances with body bags ready to take them away, and
even cages for any orphaned pets.

Dingguo is dragged out of the concrete house and pinned to the ground. 'Fuck off to Siberia, you moth-er-fucker!' he yells at the field officers. 'May your daughter freeze to death with the fucking polar bears.'

'Handcuff that wanker and shove him in the van,' says the urban-management leader, a cigarette dangling from his mouth.

The young woman who threatened to hack off Commander Zhao's penis is also pinned down and hand-cuffed. Trying to break free, she cranes her head back and sinks her teeth into the officer's arm, but is punched back down again. 'You dog-fucker,' she shouts. Seeing the big wound on his arm, the officer yells: 'You dare bite me, you filthy slut? Just wait until I get my own back on you tonight ...'

'Well, you just wait till I strap your mother to an electric fan and make her spin to death ...' Her shirt buttons have been ripped off, and her exposed breasts quiver as she howls.

'Fling that cunt into the van!' the team leader barks. A band of riot police rush over and bundle her inside.

An officer trying to detach the Xi Jinping poster is struck by a petrol can. The President's face is splashed with fuel and instantly goes up in flames. While the villagers on the street stand paralysed by fear, armed police officers brave the fire and drag people out from the concrete house. A front-loader truck advances. The elderly postman runs out and strikes an urban-management officer with an iron pick. As blood spurts from the officer's neck, an armed policeman with a shield digs an electric baton into the postman's back and kicks him to the ground.

Director Ma recalls the day East is Red attacked a hospital occupied by the Million Bold Warriors. *When we ran out of bullets, we hid behind a stack of propaganda hoardings, waited until the Million Bold Warriors had used all their hand grenades and petrol bombs, then we charged out and attacked them with farming tools. We battled all day and night, making our way up from the basement to the fourth floor. Everywhere rang with the clatter of lances, shovels and hoes. Yao Jian's square face was slashed right open along one side. He leapt on top of me and we wrestled each other to the ground. Two years before, when my classmates and I were messing about in the school corridor, Yao Jian had tried to trip me up, so I shoved him onto his back and the marbles in his pocket scattered over the concrete floor. This time, in the hospital corridor, I raised a metal hoe in the air and prepared to strike him, but he kicked it from my hands, jumped up, grabbed me by the hair, yanked my head back, pulled out a pair of scissors and pressed them against my face. I swung my fist round and punched him hard in the jaw, then wrenched the scissors from him, and with one single thrust, plunged the sharp blades into his neck. The blood that spewed from his mouth and splashed all over my face felt disgustingly warm.*

The villagers shout: 'Long live President Xi!' and then hurl petrol bombs and rocks. The demolition workers in yellow helmets begin to advance towards the village behind a line of armed police. Assistants with dogs and pitchforks rush out ahead and pursue the fleeing villagers. An elderly couple who have fallen to the ground shout: 'Long live Chairman Mao!' as they are dragged away by two female officers.

A petrol bomb strikes the red banner emblazoned: MAKE THE CHINA DREAM COME TRUE, FIGHT TO THE BITTER END TO DEFEND OUR HOMELAND! Ma Daode smells the heady petrol fumes. *The East is Red Headquarters reeked of diesel, printing ink and garlic. There were a hundred of us dossing there. When the Million Bold Warriors received a cannon from their supporters in the People's Liberation Army, they launched another attack on us. A hundred of them surrounded our headquarters, then charged up to the top floor, shouting: 'Surrender and your life will be spared!' When they reached the big room at the top, a Red Guard grabbed a boy called Cui Degen, who was standing right next to me, slammed him onto the ground, handcuffed him and struck him in the head again and again with a hand grenade until his eyes rolled back and his legs convulsed. I reached for a metal pike and rammed it into the murderer. Two other Red Guards then pounced on me and we fought with our fists until one of them stabbed me in the chest three times and I collapsed on the floor. Then Sun Tao, a boy in the year below me at school, stepped out from the gang of Million Bold Warriors, slapped my face and shouted: 'Son of Rightist dog!'*

'We'll defend President Xi with our lives!' Genzai yells to the line of shield-bearing armed police. 'Attack us, if you're not afraid to die!' A bulldozer rams into the concrete house, shattering a chunk of the facade. Afraid that the wobbling structure is about to collapse, the people on the roof drop onto their stomachs. But the sales manager Guan Dalin keeps standing, calmly strikes a match and sets himself on fire. For a few seconds he hops madly in the ball of flames, then he leaps off the roof, lands on the bulldozer and rolls onto the road. Firefighters spray him with extinguishers, and as he thrashes about in the white foam he howls: 'Long Live President Xi Jinping.' ... *One of the Million Bold Warriors boys was hit by a petrol bomb in our headquarters. We stood and watched as he jumped around in the orange flames then slowly crumpled to the ground. When his comrade went over and tried to drag his corpse outside, I raised my gun and shot him in the head.*

The bulldozer revs up again, spewing clouds of diesel smoke, and with another loud thud rams into the concrete house. 'Look over there, the construction workers are leaving the bridge and are coming over to help the villagers,' cries Commander Zhao, his face dripping in sweat.

'And those drivers are pulling up to see what's going on,' Chief Jia shouts back. 'Quick, Sergeant Pan, cordon off the area and arrest anyone who's filming on their phones.'

With a deafening crash the fake house finally caves in. Director Ma catches a final glimpse of Genzai, plummeting down in the chaos of falling concrete, his hands still clutching the national flag and the sunlight glinting on his shaven head before he disappears into the cloud of dust. He remembers that when he was digging his parents' grave in the wild grove on the other side of the river, he was gripping a Chairman Mao badge in the palm of his right hand. He glances down and sees a ripped condom, and beside it a red badge exactly like the one he is thinking about, embossed with the golden face of Chairman Mao. A brick soars overhead and hits the windscreen of a police car. Chief Jia pulls down his visor and shouts: 'Fucking hooligans!'

Waves of dust roll from the bulldozers' tracks; smells of chives and urine move through the air. Director Ma sees the middle-aged man in army camouflage being dragged towards the police van. 'Bastards!' the man shouts, foaming with rage. 'If you demolish my home I'll kill myself right here in front of you.' He has kicked off his left shoe in his effort to break free, and is digging his bare toes into the earth. His Labrador is foaming at the mouth as well.

'Fine – kill yourself if you want,' Chief Jia shouts back, infuriated that this villager has dared wear an army uniform.

'If you tear down my house, I'll murder your mother! I'll fight you to the death!' As he continues to yell, officers grab hold of his barking Labrador and lock it in a cage.

The bulldozers' tracks clank and screech. More villagers appear from a side street hoping to mount an attack, but when they see the huge column of armed police, they drop their pitchforks and flee.

Once the police manage to seize the villagers' make-shift cannons and tanks, the situation calms down. The informers in red baseball caps are arrested as well so as not to arouse suspicion. Director Ma catches a whiff of perfume from one of the captured women.

Her lipstick and streaks of dyed blonde hair turn his mind to the pleasures of the bedroom. She has a rope around her neck and is being shoved into the back of a police van by three officers.

As Ma Daode turns round and heads for the Land Cruiser, a villager bashes him with a flattened bicycle, and he tumbles onto his back with quivering legs akimbo. Hu rushes over to help him up. Commander Zhao has received a blow to the head as well and is being carried to an ambulance on a stretcher. As he passes, Director Ma grabs hold of his hand and says, 'Comrade in arms, give me your *Little Red Book*. I will take care of it. You have fallen heroically in battle. Your Red Guard armband is drenched in blood. But fear not. The East is Red flag will fly for ever over the streets of Ziyang ...'

'Let's go, Director Ma!' Hu says, trying desperately to pull him over to the car.

'Think I'm your fucking slave, do you, Ma Daode?' Commander Zhao shouts as his stretcher is pushed into the ambulance. 'Your salary's no higher than mine, you know! Making us tear down whole villages to pay for your fucking China Dream shows and your bloody China Dream Device. You fucking—' He shakes a fist in anger as the ambulance doors are closed.

'Yes, let's leave, I'm not feeling at all well,' Ma Daode says. Once inside the Land Cruiser, he takes out his mobile and reads a new text: DIRECTOR MA, DIDN'T YOU AGREE TO MEET ME FOR LUNCH AT THE PROSPERITY HOTEL? I'M WAITING FOR YOU IN ROOM 123. PLEASE HURRY UP ...

'Were you an East is Red member, by any chance, Director Ma?' Hu asks. 'I've noticed that the Cultural Revolution has been on your mind a lot these last days ...' This is the first time Hu has asked Director Ma about his past. Although his tone is casual, Director Ma spots a sly flicker in his eyes and suspects he knows more than he is letting on.

Mr Tai turns on the engine, but can't set off because the road is blocked with vehicles.

'Yes, I joined East is Red. Seeing Commander Zhao's head wrapped in bandages just now took me back to the violent struggle. In January 1968, the Million Bold Warriors attacked our headquarters in the Agricultural Machinery College. All we had were twelve rifles we'd looted from the college's military training office, but they had just been given a cannon and fifty guns by their supporters in the army. Thousands of them stormed our building and attacked us room by room, tossing hand grenades as they went. The noise was ear-splitting. When they reached the top, they tied up our vice commander and stabbed him repeatedly with two drill bits. His steaming blood and guts splattered everywhere. They called it the "Cultural Revolution". Bullshit! It was armed warfare. If auxiliary forces hadn't come to our rescue, the sixty of us held captive would have been killed. I still got stabbed three times in the chest, though. It was a miracle I survived.'

'Why rake over the past?' Hu replies, his bald head glistening with perspiration. 'You're a municipal leader now: your wish is your command. My mother died in the Cultural Revolution. She used to work for the county supply office. My father has never told me where she's buried, and I have never asked.' Hu's eyes are blank but his voice is wavering.

'We were teenagers, secondary-school children,' Ma Daode continues. 'We boycotted classes and flung ourselves into the revolution before we'd had a chance to pick sides. And once violence starts, it continues under its own momentum. First it's fists, then it's bricks, and before you know it, there will be guns. Look what happened here today, Hu – it was just like the violent struggle when opposing factions tried to kill each other while both pledging undying allegiance to Chairman Mao!' Director Ma looks out of the window at the concrete house that has been reduced to a heap of rubble. *Why was I not buried along with my comrades, all those years ago?*

'Live a worthy life and die an honourable death – that's

all we can hope for,' Mr Tai interjects. He turns the radio to a music station and taps the beat of the song on his steering wheel.

'Yes, you're right, Hu – we must forget the past. That's why I want to develop the China Dream Device. Mr Tai, can you close the windows and switch on the air conditioning, please?' Director Ma rubs the sweat from his neck with a tissue, leaving long red marks on his skin.

'Someone in the Bureau is saying that your China Dream Device is a crazy pipe dream,' Hu says, a hint of malice creeping into his voice. 'He says you're just proposing these hare-brained projects because you've run out of ideas.'

'Don't tell me who it is. Hey, Tai, pass me a cigarette.' Director Ma is troubled by what Hu has just said, but wonders whether he is telling the truth. Mayor Chen offered him a month's sabbatical last week, but he turned it down because he was afraid Hu might take over his job in his absence.

'The Cultural Revolution – it was a heroic time, though, wasn't it?' Mr Tai says. He pulls a cigarette from the car pocket, lights it and hands it to Director Ma.

'Our faith was unshakeable back then,' Director Ma replies. 'We believed that in life we followed Chairman

Mao and in death we reunited with Karl Marx. We devoted our entire being to the Communist Party. Turn left here – the road along the river is full of potholes.'

When Director Ma finishes the cigarette, he tosses it out of the window ... *I trudged for hours through dirty, broken snow. My father had sent a neighbour out to call me back home. Behind me, a man was pushing a bicycle that creaked and groaned all the way. The looted army boots I was wearing kept my feet warm. When I opened our front door I smelt chicken stew. My sister was by the stove, stirring a pot of corn gruel. There were feathers and drops of chicken blood on the floor. On a chair in the corner was a placard that said:* DOWN WITH EVIL RIGHTIST MA LEI *and a tall, cone-shaped dunce's hat. My father was sitting on the bed under a lamp, writing a letter. He glanced up and noticed the bandages around my head. When we had attacked a convention of rebel factions the day before, a soldier guarding the rostrum had hit me with his rifle butt. My mother came out from under the door curtain with a basin of hot water disinfected with purple potassium permanganate. She told my father to stretch out his legs. His bloodied kneecaps were splintered with fine shards of coal. My mother whispered to me: 'Come and help hold up his knees, Daode,' but I ignored her. She washed Father's knees with the disinfected water until her hands were stained purple. My father shuddered at the pain, but didn't make a sound. Through the corners of his eyes, he continued to look at the letter he was writing. That afternoon, Red Guards had forced him to kneel in hot coal ashes. But I had drawn a clear political line between myself and this old Rightist called Ma Lei, so I could not allow myself to help my mother treat his wounds.*

A hot breeze blows in through the car window. Director Ma presses the button to close it again. *With the big white bandage around my head and a look of surly resentment, I knelt by the stove and pumped the bellows to keep the fire going, and glanced briefly at my father wiping his face with a flannel. 'As long as the wounds are clean I'll be fine,' he said to my mother. The flannel was drenched with his blood and sweat. The more he wiped his neck with it, the dirtier his neck became.*

The scent of the chicken stew softened the room's hard edges. I asked my sister to tell me who had done this to our father. She dropped some salt into the pot and picked up some chopped spring onions. 'It was another struggle session, of course,' she answered at last. 'I hope one day that boy will know what it's like to kneel on hot ashes with a heavy placard around his neck. Here, Mother, have this.' She sprinkled the bowl of corn gruel with the chopped spring onions and handed it to my mother, then ladled some out for me. I drank it ravenously, blowing on each spoonful to stop it burning my mouth.

'I have some spare bandages,' I said, careful not to look at anyone in particular.

'I'm fine – let's all go to sleep now,' my father said. 'You've walked a long way. Have a quick wash, then go to bed.' Although he didn't raise his eyes, I knew he was talking to me. I wondered why he had called me home if it was just to have a meal and go to bed. My mother told me to take off my dirty socks and boil up some water for my father. I wanted to shout at her, but was too tired. I had spent months living on the streets, fighting endless battles, and there was seldom a chance to sleep. The Million Bold Warriors had seized control of the outskirts. We had captured four of Ziyang's fourteen schools and most of the hospitals, post offices and department stores, but had lost many lives in clashes near the train station and the Drum Tower. As soon as I stretched out on the sofa I was overcome with exhaustion and sank into a deep sleep.

In my dreams, I heard my father moan like an ox. My sister shook me awake and shouted: 'Get up. Mother and Father have locked themselves in the attic!' I ran upstairs and banged on the door. I smelt a strong whiff of pesticide seeping through the cracks. 'Open the door,' my sister pleaded. 'What are you two doing in there?' She burst into *tears, and kept knocking, again and again. I heard fingernails scraping against the floorboards inside. I wanted to light a lamp. My sister groped her way downstairs in the dark and ran to the back yard. Then she called out and told me to come outside, climb up to the attic and smash the window. I did as she asked. After clambering inside, I switched on the light and saw my parents on the floor, my mother's purple-stained hand gripping my father's sallow hand, as their souls drifted off to the Yellow Springs of the netherworld. Beside my father lay an opened bottle of pesticide. The foul liquid that was leaking from it smelt like raw garlic and paraffin. An enamel wash bowl my mother had used to clean her face lay toppled beside her in a puddle of water.*

Director Ma feels his grief weighing down like an overripe pear that longs to drop from its branch but is afraid of smashing into pieces. The Land Cruiser approaches Drum Tower Street in the old quarter of Ziyang. White Heaven is on the next turning to the left. He will enter through the Gate of Heavenly Peace, update Propaganda Chief Ding on the morning's events and proceed to Prosperity Hotel. After a quick talk with the general manager about the Golden Anniversary Dream, he will then check into a room and make love to his new mistress. She is a young woman who has returned from America with a business degree, and now calls herself 'Claire'. He met her ten days ago when she came to the China Dream Bureau and proposed to help them set up a giant advertising screen somewhere in the city centre.

Dreaming your life away in a drunken haze

Director Ma walks into the reception hall of the Red Guard Nightclub. Pink and red lanterns cast a rosy glow over Maoist propaganda boards and Red Guard flags. Young hostesses wearing the green military uniforms and red armbands of the Cultural Revolution line up in front of him. His pulse quickens; he feels sixteen again. He removes his sunglasses, goes over to Number 8 and nods. After she has informed him that her measurements are 80, 60, 75, he takes her hand, says: 'I'll have you tonight,' and leads her to Chairman Mao's private compartment. He spotted the name of this club on a list of establishments targeted in a recent campaign against pornography, and decided to try it out himself tonight instead of sleeping with one of his many mistresses.

'What's the hurry, Chief? Sit down and have a drink

with me. I'll open this bottle of French claret to welcome you to our club.' Number 8 squeezes Director Ma's hand, half cajoling him, half pushing him away. This room is a mock-up of an official train compartment used by Mao Zedong. There is a desk with pencils, a fountain pen and an ashtray; a hanging scroll inscribed with a line of Mao's poetry: A CAVE CREATED FOR IMMORTALS, / FROM THE PEAKS THE VIEW IS SUBLIME; a sofa, an armchair, a pair of slippers and a silk dressing gown. It even has a replica carriage window that looks out onto a large coloured poster of the green terraced rice fields of Mao's model village, Dazhai.

'Tonight, young lady, you will play the part of my first love. Let me look at you. Ah, hands as slender as blades of grass, skin as yielding as congealed fat, neck white as a maggot, eyebrows delicate as the wings of a black moth ...' With great delight, Director Ma removes the hostess's red-starred military cap, sinks into the armchair and fills two glasses with claret.

'I'm like moths and maggots?' Number 8 says indignantly. She watches Ma Daode swig back his drink, then downs hers in one as well.

'I'm quoting a poem from the *Book of Odes*,' Ma Daode answers, gazing up at the ceiling light. 'It's a eulogy of a beautiful woman. You should read more widely.'

'But moths and maggots – that's a bit disgusting, isn't

it?' Number 8 wrinkles her nose and tucks her hair behind her ears. Under the glow of the red lamp her face looks plastic.

'With decoration like this, I expect they'll charge me two thousand five hundred yuan for the room, two thousand to sleep with you, and another thousand if I don't use a condom,' Ma Daode says. Then raising his eyebrows suggestively he whispers: 'The sluttier you behave the larger your tip!' He strokes her hair, then puts a lock of it in his mouth and sucks. 'Mm. You've just washed it, haven't you? Delicious!' Then he unbuttons her green army jacket and snaps open her bra. 'Ah, so round and ample. Two pillows of pale pink alabaster ...' A wave of pleasure surges to his throat. 'Come, let your vermilion lips blow my amethyst flute ...'

He pushes her head to his groin and drips some claret onto her lips. 'Tonight I will be Ximen Qing, the corrupt and lustful merchant from *The Plum in the Golden Vase*. That's a book you should read. It's a classic work of erotic fiction. Lots of explicit passages. In the Cultural Revolution, Mao only allowed high officials to read the unabridged version ...' He observes her for a while, then leans back, stretches out his legs and reads the subtitles of the karaoke video showing on the flat screen attached to the wall: DEAREST CHAIRMAN MAO, YOU ARE ALWAYS IN OUR HEARTS. WHEN WE ARE LOST, YOU

SHOW US THE WAY. WHEN WE ARE PLUNGED IN DARK- NESS, YOU LIGHT UP OUR PATH ... He turns up the volume, closes his eyes and mumbles: 'With her gentle teeth, soft tongue and delicate hands she caresses the jade stalk ... Now I am Chairman Mao sitting in his private carriage, and you are Zhang Yufeng, his personal train attendant.'

Kneeling in front of the armchair, Number 8 raises her head and with a look of misty admiration says: 'Yes, Chief. Every day you attend to countless state affairs for the sake of humanity. It is our revolutionary duty to ensure that tonight you enjoy a good rest.'

'Sounds like you know a lot about the Cultural Revolution, then?' Director Ma asks, dropping his official tone. He looks at the Mao portrait and feels proud to have gained admission to the Chairman's private space. A stream of pleasure flows through his veins.

'Not really – what was it exactly?' Number 8 asks, looking up again, a pubic hair stuck to the corner of her mouth and her lipstick smudged up to her nostrils.

'The Great Proletarian Cultural Revolution. Surely your parents have mentioned it to you!' Now that Director Ma has removed all of his clothes, his voice has acquired a playful, sing-song tone.

'Well, I know this uniform's from the Cultural Revolution, isn't it?' She leans down over his crotch again, and her black hair sways about as her head moves back and forth, back and forth.

'Yes, that's a Red Guard uniform. But you should have the name of your faction on your armband. "East is Red Combat Team", for example. The Red Guards were not much younger than you. Mao saw them as his little soldiers and told them to "create great disorder under Heaven". When factory workers joined the movement, they split into rival factions and the violence spiralled out of control ...' As soon as Director Ma starts pontificating, his penis goes soft. Number 8 removes it from her mouth and slowly rubs it back to life with her pink manicured fingers.

'I don't care if I'm wearing the correct uniform or not. Our boss told us we are all the heirs of Communism.'

As he swallows some more claret, Director Ma sees his childhood sweetheart, Pan Hua, appear in his mind's eye, dressed in a khaki army jacket with a white, sewn-on collar. *'Be kind to your mother when you get home,' she told me before I left the headquarters. 'Take my copy of Mao's* Little Red Book *with you. It will keep you safe on your journey.' My heart started beating so fast, all I could say in reply was: 'I'll be back tomorrow.' But my parents committed suicide that night, and when I returned to the East is Red headquarters a week later, I learned that Pan Hua had been killed in a battle ...* Director Ma feels a cold draught blow across his spine. He wraps his legs around Number 8's waist and sits up, trying to pull his fat belly in.

Through half-open eyes he watches Number 8's naked breasts wobble up and down as she rubs his jade stalk with a hot flannel. 'What time do you go home?' he asks, staring now at a lock of hennaed hair dangling across her face.

'I clock off at midnight, Chief, and start again at seven in the morning. Would you like another service from me?'

'Well, I haven't screwed you yet. But why don't we have a chat first. Come and sit next to me and let's get to know each other a little better. Now, you will be Comrade Pan Hua.'

'Fine, Chief. Which club does Pan Hua work in? Does she look like me? I'm one metre seventy tall.'

'She's in ... Heaven.' He leans back in the armchair and looks up at the ceiling.

'I know that place – the Heaven on Earth Club. All the girls who work there have college degrees.' Her lock of hennaed hair is now sticking up like a red cockscomb.

'I mean she's in Heaven, not on Earth.' In a grandfatherly tone he continues: 'I loved the film *Battle for Yan'an* and the Russian novel, *Anna Karenina*. But Pan Hua had

never read a book in her life – she only liked magazines.'
He downs another glass of claret, puts a few raisins in
his mouth and feels a craving for a cigarette. The subtitles
of another song appear on the screen: I DONATE MY
PETROLEUM TO THE MOTHERLAND. / AS IT GUSHES
FROM MY WELLS, FLOWERS OF JOY BLOOM FROM MY
HEART.

*I don't know whether Pan Hua ever sang these songs.
I don't even know how tall she was. I do know that she
wore her hair in two plaits tied with red wool, and, just
like Number 8 here, had a Chairman Mao badge on her
chest, a red armband on her sleeve and a military belt
buckled tightly around her waist. She also wore a red
scarf. But I have no idea what her fingers, feet, neck or
breasts looked like. We were both members of East is Red
and even drank from the same Thermos flask, but the
truth is I knew very little about her ...* Ma Daode feels
light-headed now that the alcohol is coursing through
his bloodstream ... *My family and I lived in Yaobang for
only six months during the Great Famine, and I was just
eight years old. But some memories of that time are still
vivid. I remember seeing villagers peeling the bark from
trees and eating it to fend off starvation. And I remember
seeing the mother of Tianmu, a little girl I used to walk
to the village school with, sitting on her porch, stone dead,
her hands still gripping an empty bowl. If my father hadn't*

been called back to Ziyang to oversee research into protein-rich algae, I doubt our family would have survived.

Fondling Number 8's breasts with one hand, Director Ma scrolls through his messages with the other. He finds one from his daughter in England: HI DAD, GUESS WHO I SAW IN LONDON TODAY? ONLY OUR PRESIDENT, PAPA XI, AND HIS WIFE, MAMA PENG! WHEN THEY PASSED BY IN THE QUEEN'S GOLDEN CARRIAGE, MY FRIENDS AND I HELD UP HUGE CHINESE FLAGS OVER SOME PLACARDS ABOUT THE SO-CALLED TIANANMEN MASSACRE. THEY WERE FULL OF LIES, OF COURSE, COOKED UP BY FOREIGN REACTIONARIES SEEKING TO HAMPER CHINA'S RISE. THERE WERE SOME TIBETANS THERE AS WELL, WAVING SEPARATIST FLAGS. AND THE ENGLISH POLICE DIDN'T EVEN TRY TO ARREST THEM. CAN YOU BELIEVE IT? Ma Daode combs his fingers through Number 8's hair and pushes her head back down between his legs. Then he leans back, turns up the volume with the remote control and sings along with the revolutionary song, tapping out the rhythm on Number 8's back: '"The Communist Party summons us to join the revolution. Gladly we seize the whip and strike our enemies down ..."' Recalling what a flat arse he had as a young man, he takes Number 8's hand and presses it against his buttocks. 'Feel this arse of mine. Isn't it fat? Isn't it round? I'm just so fucking perfect!' Thinking back to his youth again, he says: 'My wife was perfect as well. She was as beautiful as a lotus flower. I used to gladly finish off the baked potato skins she'd leave on the side of her plate.'

'And look how big and hard this is,' Number 8 says, weighing his penis in her hand, trying to prolong the conversation so as to give her mouth a rest. 'What's that?' she asks, touching a scar on his chest. 'Did you have an operation?'

'See, there's another one here, and here. I was stabbed three times by the Red Guards.'

'So you really are a hero of the revolution!' Number 8 exclaims, looking up with wonder. Her face is slightly darker than her shoulders.

'My wife's brother was a Red Guard. He belonged to a rival faction. In one battle we stole four of their jeeps. Huh, who would have guessed I'd end up marrying his little sister ...' Ma Daode feels his guard lowering further now that the alcohol has fully kicked in. 'Let's turn on the news,' he says, 'Well, look at that headline: "Former Party Secretary of Chongqing, Bo Xilai, has today been sentenced to life in prison for bribery, embezzlement and abuse of power." Fuck me! That old Red Guard's had it this time!' Ma Daode looks like a stout, hairless pig now, as he sits slouched in the armchair, sucking on a cigarette, his knees knocking together.

'My mouth is sore, Chief. Can't you just finish off inside me?' Although Number 8 is exhausted, she still manages a placating smile.

'All right, my dear Pan Hua, I'll take care of you.' Without further ado, he heaves himself out of the chair, presses her against the sofa and pulls off her black nylon tights. Then he grabs a breast in each hand and gently rocks her from side to side in the 'wandering dragon toys with the phoenix' position. The old photograph of Chairman Mao on the wall in front of him sways from left to right. 'My darling Pan Hua, were you just a dream, or am I dreaming now?' Sliding into a half-trance, he starts to pull her back and forth as though rowing a boat, first with leisurely strokes, then with increasing force until, brimming with desire and gasping for breath, he discharges into her, his legs jolting spasmodically like an ejaculating stud horse.

Ma Daode only started being unfaithful to his wife after he became County Propaganda Chief. Before long, he was sleeping with a different woman every night, as though he was working his way through a tray of regional snacks. At first, he took cuttings of their pubic hair to keep as souvenirs, but soon collected so many that he couldn't tell which ones belonged to whom, so he locked them all up in a drawer and abandoned the habit. Now that the years have caught up with him, he has resolved to have just twelve mistresses at any one time, and has even considered limiting himself to six, because making love every day takes its toll on his health.

Director Ma sniffs the smell of Number 8's sweat on his fingers and gazes at her white teeth sparkling behind her ruffled hair. 'Bet not even you enjoyed such a blissful time as this, Chairman Mao!' he says with a grin, his breath pungent with alcohol. 'Quick! Tell the boss to send me two more!'

Moments later, five girls enter the room. Without being asked, two of them approach Director Ma and stroke his shoulders and pot belly. 'Fine, I'll have these two: Number Six and Number Ten. Take your clothes off and lie down over there.' He points to the large sofa on which Number 8 is sitting. The three girls who weren't chosen quietly leave the room.

'Why don't we book a hotel room instead, Chief?' asks Number 10. 'It will be quieter there.'

'You're afraid the police will raid the club? Don't worry. In Ziyang, what I say goes. Now hurry up and strip.' For a few minutes he sits on the armchair and watches the undulating curves of six soft breasts dance before his eyes. Then, unable to restrain himself, he crawls over, kneels on the rug and inserts himself repeatedly into the dark thicket between Number 8's legs, using the ancient thrusting method of 'nine shallow, one deep'. Resting his head on Number 6's thighs, he slides his right hand up Number 10's plump belly and traces circles around her nipple with his fingertips. When he hears her moan, he withdraws his jade stalk from Number 8 and thrusts it into Number 10's peony blossom, opening the petals with his fingers to ease it in, then quickly pushes his left hand, adorned with a Swiss watch, back into Number 8's thicket. Moving his right hand over to caress Number 6's pink crevice, he extracts his shaft, moistens it with a drop of saliva, then rams it into Number 8 again, entering her in upward and downward strokes, then in a winding, circular pattern, each time venturing deeper into the dark interior of her jade-white body until, ascending to a peak of pleasure, shuddering and groaning, he ejects another batch of his vital essence. His energy spent, he leans over for another glug of wine, then curls up like a prawn on a hot grill, nestling himself between Number 8's willowy waist and Number 10's plump belly.

'What a stud you are, Chief, spurting one load after another, at your age!' says Number 8, clenching her thighs together. The beige nylon bra she is clutching looks like a bunch of withered flowers.

'Yes, it's my secret golden rifle,' he mumbles with half-shut eyes, feeling his flesh spreading out like soft clay.

'He's leaked onto the rug – quick, get some paper and wipe it up,' Number 10 says to the other two as she reaches down for her knickers. She is wearing only knee-high boots. She stands up brusquely. As she catches her breath, her breasts and belly rise and fall.

'I'm sick of these red songs,' Director Ma says. 'Can't you put on some pop music instead?' Feeling drowsy and dazed, he stares at the light flashing on his mobile phone and wishes he could crawl off into some dark, faraway place he has never been before.

'Chairman Mao's private carriage only has songs from the revolution,' says Number 10, reaching behind her back to do up her bra. The hair in her armpits reminds Ma Daode of his oldest lover Li Wei. Last time he went to bed with her he couldn't get an erection however hard he tried.

'Revolution, huh!' he says, rousing himself a little. 'Do you realise that in Chinese the literal meaning of the revolution is "to sever life". Well, when I was a teenager, I severed three lives while singing revolutionary songs. That was before any of you were born.' The screen on the wall appears to be shaking. Although he knows he has drunk too much, he still accepts another glass of wine from Number 8 and swallows half of it in one gulp. When it reaches his stomach, he sees a cloud of purple sparks.

Number 10 drapes a khaki army coat over her shoulders, leaves the room and returns with a tray of fruit and hot flannels. Ma Daode stares at the exposed strip of skin stretching from her foot to the top of her thigh. The name of a popular rap folksong appears on the screen, and when the music starts, he sings along with the subtitles: '"I gaze to that magical place above the moon and wonder how many dreams are floating there …"' Numbers 6 and 10, who are now seated on either side of him with Red Guard jackets over their shoulders, join in, singing loudly and from the heart. Number 8 is cross-legged on the rug in an unbuttoned khaki coat, a gold chain sparkling over her cleavage. Four black stilettos lie in a heap beside her.

'Bring me another tray of fruit – Taiwanese mangoes and Thai lychees,' Ma Daode commands. 'And tell me what faction you Red Guards belong to. Tell me, or I'll shoot you dead!'

'Calm down,' Number 6 smiles, pulling a dirty plaster from her toe. 'We're just regular Red Guards offering our bodies to senior officials. We don't belong to any faction.'

'Impossible!' he says, jabbing Number 10's armband so hard he spills his wine onto his lap. 'Every Red Guard had to choose a side! When I was sixteen, I killed a boy who was one metre eighty tall, simply because his faction wasn't as revolutionary as ours. Anyone who opposed us was our enemy.'

'Let's open some more claret, Chief. I'll help you drink it.' Ma Daode sees Number 10's white buttocks clench as she expertly uncorks another bottle.

'No more wine,' Number 6 says to her. 'Our guest is a wealthy CEO, didn't you know? A big shot! Open a bottle of Maotai, and let me show him how charming I can be when I have some liquor inside me.' Number 6 gives Ma Daode a coy smile and slips her hand between his legs. As he stares at her red lips and white teeth he catches glimpses of tender moments from his past.

'I can't tell you who I am, of course, but I am not a CEO,' he says, trying hard to sound sober. 'All right, open a bottle of Maotai, if you insist. It's only eighteen thousand yuan! I know very well what you're up to, tricking me into buying expensive drinks!' He unzips his black purse and pulls out a wad of notes printed with the red portrait of Chairman Mao. 'I will defend the China Dream to the death!' he exclaims as he hands the wad to Number 8. The other two Red Guards on the sofa pounce on her, and the three of them wrestle to the floor, then start scampering about like chickens, trying to pick up the fallen notes ... *A paper tiger is chasing me along a dark mountain path. Its eyes blaze like torches. Just as it's about to pounce on me, I see my father's broad face and large ears. His mouth is wide open and twisted to one side* ... Ma Daode is woken by the ringing of his phone. 'Bring me the most expensive bottle!' he cries out into the empty room. 'Bring me the most beautiful ...' Then he closes his eyes and sinks back into his dream.

Life floats by like a dream

Autumn rain splatters onto the road. The early-morning sky is bright but seems imbued with a cold misery. Director Ma, dressed in a dark blue suit, climbs into his official car. Today the 'China Dream: Golden Anniversary Dream' ceremony will take place in Garden Square in the newly expanded Yaobang Industrial Park. This is the most important event Ma Daode has overseen since becoming director of the China Dream Bureau. He reminds himself not to stray from his prepared speech. If he wants to retain his position until retirement, he can't afford to let his mind wander again. He repeats the five-word mantra his mistress Li Wei taught him to banish his past self from his mind: 'You're not me. Go away. You're not me. Go away.'

Mr Tai, the driver, switches on the radio: 'Thanks to the new spirit of enterprise fostered by Yaobang Industrial

Park, Golden Cow Dairy Company has won first prize in the county's technological innovation competition ...'

'Turn it down, I want to check my voicemails,' says Director Ma, flicking through his phone. The first message informs him that Xu An, head of Ziyang Complaints Department, has committed suicide in his office, and that the public have started discussion threads about his death in the comment section of the China Dream Bureau website. Director Ma knows that this kind of negative news item must be suppressed immediately. The second message relays the disappointing news that finance for the China Dream Device has still not been approved. 'Have we hit a traffic jam?' he asks, without looking up. 'Put the siren on the roof.'

'No, that won't help,' Mr Tai answers. 'Mayor Chen is cycling to work this morning and the road ahead's been closed for him since eight o'clock.'

'Oh, yes – how could I forget? The police did a security sweep last night to make sure his route is safe.' A second later, Director Ma hears a loud siren and sees eight beautiful policewomen on motorbikes drive slowly past. Then Mayor Chen himself appears, pedalling along in shorts and a white Aertex shirt, his plump belly bulging like a penguin's, flanked on both sides by four more policewomen and followed by an ambulance and a television camera van. The people who have gathered to watch gasp with disbelief and beam with admiration, amazed by his vitality and vigour.

'What a happy scene – a great example of positive interaction between the leaders and the masses,' Director Ma says to Mr Tai. Immediately he remembers the euphoric crowd who paraded down this road in the Cultural Revolution, holding aloft huge mangoes made of papier mâché, in honour of the mangoes that Chairman Mao had given days before to a group of Beijing factory workers who had pacified overzealous Red Guards at Qinghua University. The jubilant crowd understood that Mao's gift of fruit signified the end of the violent struggle. Director Ma pushes that scene out of his mind, looks out through the window again and says: 'So, Mr Tai, do you think I will have to cycle to work from now on?'

'Don't worry,' Mr Tai replies, starting up the engine. 'Mayor Chen's just doing this for show. It will be all over the evening news tonight, then he'll be back in his chauffeured limousine tomorrow.' He too is gazing at the three policewomen on motorbikes driving in front of them as they follow the Mayor's cavalcade all the way to White Heaven.

As soon as Ma Daode enters the lift, a long-forgotten quote returns to him: *'At the first sound of gunfire, I will charge. Today, I will perish on the battlefield ...'* *Why has that quotation from Marshall Lin Biao wormed its way back into my mind? I remember kneeling on a street, head bowed, in front of a Red Guard who was in a class above me at school, blubbering: 'I surrender, big brother.' But the boy next to him still bashed me on the head with a club and shouted: 'I'll murder you, you son of a Rightist dog.'*

'Are you dreaming you're back on the battlefield, Ma Daode?' Song Bin asks with a mocking sneer. His face always looks sallow and puffy in the morning. Ma Daode has heard that Song Bin's wife wants to open a branch of the Qingfeng Dumpling Store. 'Looks like the China Dream really is producing miracles!' Song Bin says to the others in the lift. 'Our Director Ma here keeps composing the most wonderful dream poems. Look at this one he's just posted on WeChat: FORGETTING IS THE ALLY OF REAL DREAMS. / REAL DREAMS ARE THE ENEMY OF FORGETTING. / YOU ARE THE DREAM WITHIN MY DREAM. I AM THE—'

Director Ma flashes Song Bin a frosty smile and walks out through the opening doors. Then he hurries to his office, closes the door, sinks into the black leather sofa and buries his head in his hands.

He wants a few moments of peace to decide what to do about his conflicting selves. *Yes, I must kill one of them off. My past self, of course. But how do I eradicate the past? My China Dream Device won't be in production for months. I can't wait that long: these two Ma Daodes are locked in combat and will destroy each other before then. As far as I know, only the dead are able to permanently forget the past, when they drink Old Lady Dream's Broth of Amnesia in the netherworld, before they are reincarnated in a new body. Of course! That's what I need. I must get the recipe at once . . .* 'Broth of Amnesia!' Director Ma cries out, looking as though he's just woken from a long sleep. 'Come into my office, Hu! I want you to call Master Wang Lin, the snake-conjurer and Qigong healer, and invite him to this afternoon's Golden Anniversary Dream.' When Ma Daode's protruding eyes are wide open, he looks exactly like a toad.

'You do realise that Master Wang is a frequent guest of Mayor Chen?' Hu says with a hint of condescension.

'I don't care what you have to pay him, just make sure he comes. Tell him he'll be my VIP guest.' Now that Ma Daode has fixed on a plan, his five viscera and six entrails relax. He picks up a file from his desk and skims through it. It's a report by the head of the Internet Monitoring Unit on the China Dream Bureau's collaboration with Number 3 Jail. The Bureau pays the jail 300 yuan a month to ensure that a selected group of inmates regularly deletes any negative comments from the Bureau's website and replaces them with positive ones. Last month, however, two of the inmates attached graphic photographs of crash victims, which they had uploaded from social media, to a short piece about a high-speed train disaster. To prevent such mistakes recurring, the report recommends that the Bureau employs one hundred administrators to regularly check the prisoners' political records. On the report's final page, Director Ma writes: I AGREE. SUBMIT TO THE PROPAGANDA DEPARTMENT FOR APPROVAL.

At midday, Director Ma's car pulls up at the exact spot where three months ago the concrete house was demolished. The Buddha Light Temple is still standing, but the rest of Yaobang has been flattened and turned into a temporary car park. Director Ma recalls again the sight of shaven-headed Genzai plummeting to his death in a cloud of concrete dust. Last week, Liu Qi gave Director Ma a red envelope containing 10,000 yuan, hoping he would help get her father, Dingguo, released from detention, as her family could not afford the 150 yuan a day the police charged for his food and lodging. But for the first time in his life Ma Daode refused to take the bribe. He wants to make sure his own future is safe before agreeing to help anyone else.

A few elderly couples who have arrived early climb out of their limousines and go to chat with the welcoming hostesses. The bridal boutique owned by Ma Daode's new mistress, Claire, has delivered tailor-made wedding clothes and placed them in a pile, ready to be handed out. The Golden Anniversary Dream ceremony is being held here to coincide with the grand opening of the steel bridge over the Fenshui River. In honour of today's romantic event, the Municipal Party Committee has named it Magpie Bridge, after the legendary bridge spanning the Milky Way where two mythical lovers embrace once a year. The ribbon tied across the entrance to the bridge will be cut at the start of the ceremony.

Director Ma is taken aback by the lavish decorations. The bridge is laid with red carpet and adorned with a huge welcome arch made of baubles and flowers that are even brighter than the blue sky above. Claire has done an excellent job. In fifty minutes' time, the elderly couples will follow the red carpet under the arch, cross the bridge and proceed into Garden Square, which is festooned with silk garlands and colourful balloons.

The square has been built directly above the former burial ground. A solitary willow is all that remains of the wild grove. It is an ancient tree with gnarled and jagged branches that stab out in all directions.

Director Ma knows that beneath the concrete slabs around this willow lie the dead bodies of his parents, and of his comrades and enemies who slaughtered each other for the sake of Mao Zedong Thought. Once again

he remembers hearing his father mutter wearily: 'I'm fine
– let's all go to sleep now,' before flicking down the light
switch. *As I sank into slumber on the sofa, I could still
hear my mother and sister talking: 'We should wash your
father's feet …' 'I'll boil up some water, then …' 'Is there
enough in the pot? …' 'Yes, there's enough. Don't get up
…'* Ma Daode smells once more the stench of suicide.
When he looks at the ancient willow basking in the
October sunlight, he feels his heart grow as cold as the
roots clawing into the earth.

As the military band strikes up the song 'You Are my
Walking Stick', a procession of elderly couples, the
women in white wedding robes and the men in red
brocade suits, begin to walk hand in hand beneath the
ceremonial arch and continue slowly across the bridge.
Some of the old women are wearing silver tiaras and red
court shoes, like princesses from European fairy tales.
Others are hunched over and tottering along on crutches,
with thick jumpers over their white robes. The men on
their right form a long strip of grey heads dotted with a
few bald scalps and black top hats. Their traditional red
brocade suits complement their wives' white gowns in a
harmonious union of East and West. One old woman
sees a daisy from her floral headpiece fall onto the carpet
and tries to reach down to pick it up, but trips on her
veil and falls over, bringing her elderly husband down

with her. The ceremonial arch stands before them like the gates of paradise. Ma Daode's eyes moisten as he watches the elderly couples advance towards it. Claire and the women in red air-stewardess uniforms hand each of them a red rose as they pass.

Although everything is going to plan, Ma Daode is breaking into a nervous sweat, not because Claire, Yuyu and his wife are all present and observing him closely, but because since these one hundred elderly couples have begun to parade past him, his other self has started assaulting his mind with slogans and scenes from his youth.

In the middle of the night, my sister and I dragged my parents' coffin all the way from Ziyang in a rickety wooden handcart. When we finally arrived here, my sister fell to her knees in exhaustion. We dug into the earth below the trees until we reached the water level. The coffin was too heavy for us to lift off the cart. We thought of pulling my mother's body out and burying her first, but we couldn't unclasp her fingers from my father's hand, so in the end we pushed the coffin into the grave with both bodies squashed inside it. The scene replays so vividly before Director Ma's eyes that he is convinced this place is still haunted by the spirits of the dead.

He slowly climbs onto the podium, then lifts his head to the blue sky and commences his speech: 'Like the autumn breeze, now warm, now cold, life has its joys and sorrows. Today, though, is a beautiful day. The glorious China Dream has at last become a reality. Look at the magnificent ceremonial arch. It must be the largest of its kind in the world. And look at this multitude of elderly, wrinkled faces, beaming with hope and joy!' After a brief pause, he bellows: 'Let the Golden Anniversary Dream begin!' *Thank goodness my past self didn't mess that up*, he says to himself, then repeats his mantra: *You're not me. Go away. You're not me. Go away . . .*

While the military band strikes up again, leaders from every level of the Municipal Party Committee together with foreign businessmen from the Yaobang Industrial Park take their seats on the podium. The Buddha Light Temple on the opposite bank is encased in scaffolding and plastic sheeting. From a distance it looks like the excavation site of an ancient tomb. Arching above it like a bloodstained rainbow is a red banner proclaiming: THE ONLY WAY TO MAKE THE CHINA DREAM COME TRUE IS TO FAITHFULLY FOLLOW THE CHINESE COMMUNIST PARTY. One elderly couple after another, now accompanied on each side by a child, circles a giant wedding cake encrusted with fondant roses, then steps onto the podium to receive a souvenir badge from Mayor Chen.

An elderly man who has been chosen to speak on

behalf of the participating couples says into the microphone: 'Honoured guests, I am eighty-one years old, and my wife here is seventy-six. We have walked through life together for fifty-two years. On our wedding day, we had a simple meal with some close friends and received one bed, two bedspreads, three jin of pumpkin seeds and four jin of sweets – and that was the end of it. Never in our wildest dreams could we have imagined that when we reached our golden anniversary, we would be treated to such a sumptuous, Western-style wedding. If only our daughter were here, everything would be perfect.'

His wife, dressed in a dazzling white gown and with pink rouge on her cheeks, walks over to the microphone and interjects: 'I am overwhelmed with emotion. We always dreamed of giving our only child a grand wedding like this. Since she died, my husband and I have suffered years of grief. So we can't believe our good fortune that today we are able to participate in this beautiful, romantic ceremony. '

His eyes welling up, Director Ma walks over to these two kind souls and says: 'My dearest mother and father, you have woken up inside the China Dream and have returned to me at last!' Then he pinches himself and says: 'What I mean is: you may have lost your only child, but don't be sad, because now you are parents to us all!' Before asking this couple to speak today, he checked their political backgrounds to ensure that they are both reliable Party members.

When the old man slips a gold ring onto his wife's wrinkled finger, she cries out: 'My dream has come true!' and the crowd bursts into applause.

Director Ma raises his microphone again to say: 'Let us thank the relevant leaders for allowing these parents to realise their China Dream, and thank our foreign sponsors for their generous support. Fifty years ago this place was a mass grave filled with nameless bodies, but today it is a Garden Square on which we celebrate golden anniversaries! The China Dream eradicates all dreams of the past and replaces them with brand-new dreams! As I look out at your smiling faces, I can't help think of my own mother and father who lie buried in the ground beneath us. Sadly, the relentless struggle sessions they were subjected to proved too much for them to bear, so they are not able to join us today.' As more tears fill his eyes, he tries to snap back to his senses. 'Of course, the past must be buried before the future can be forged. Only then can our dreams come true. Only then can young people experience the beauty of love ...'

'Our daughter was murdered in the violent struggles of the Cultural Revolution,' the old man says, his voice ringing out like a bell. 'I'm so sad she's not here to share this day with us.'

'What was her name?' Director Ma asks through the screeching microphone, looking searchingly into the man's eyes. He thinks he belongs to the Municipal Committee of the People's Political Consultative Conference.

'Her name was Pan Hua. I am Pan Qiang.' The old man points to the name badge on his lapel. Every eye in the audience focuses on him.

'I don't believe it!' Director Ma gasps. 'Dear comrade, I knew your daughter well! The last time I saw her, she gave me her copy of the *Little Red Book*. I still have it in my drawer. We have ... s-s-so much ... to talk about ... I ...' Director Ma stutters and stalls, struggling to express all that he wants to say. Before he has reached the end of his sentence, two security guards jump onto the podium and order him to step down. When his feet touch the ground, he suddenly catches sight of his parents' bodies. They are not under the ancient willow after all, but further away, nearer the river. He remembers now that when he and his sister were digging the grave, it was so dark they could barely see a thing. It was only after they had buried the bodies and walked some distance through the grove that the moon briefly emerged from the clouds and he caught sight of this willow's jagged branches stabbing the night air.

Chief Ding takes over proceedings. 'Dear compatriots and elders,' he says. 'Why are we promoting the China Dream? For a better tomorrow! And today's Golden Anniversary Dream is one further step along our path. Now, let's continue with the ceremony. The band will play us a final song and then the Ziyang Dance Troupe will perform their new ballet, *The Qingfeng Dumpling Store*. After that, you will all be invited to take your seats at the wedding banquet.'

A man in a white suit appears on the podium and sings: '"Your smile is as sweet as blossom opening its petals in the spring breeze …"' Director Ma is placed in the back of a police car. As it speeds off towards Ziyang, he rests his head on the window and listens to the Golden Anniversary Dream fade into the distance.

Beguiled by empty pipe dreams

A few days later, after being suspended from his job for his bizarre and erratic behaviour, and for mentioning the Cultural Revolution during the Golden Anniversary Dream ceremony, Director Ma is sitting on a green sofa in the living room of the renowned Qigong healer, Master Wang. He has seen a documentary about him on television, and knows that this is the best position from which to watch him conjure snakes from thin air. He also knows that during the 1983 campaign against 'spiritual pollution', Master Wang was jailed for dancing cheek to cheek with a woman.

'Please help me, Master Wang,' Director Ma says. 'I'll be sixty-two this year. I thought my troubles were all behind me. But in the last few months, forgotten episodes from my youth keep jumping back into my mind, disturbing me so much that my job is now under threat.

When I open my mouth, I start spouting words I said when I was sixteen, and past events unfold before my eyes as though they are happening right now.' Ma Daode has dropped the authoritative tone of voice he employs as a government leader.

'You wait until you're suspended before you seek my assistance?' Master Wang chuckles, his small pointed chin jutting out. 'You obviously don't regard me very highly.' His head is completely bald apart from a few straggly strands of hair. Against the pale skin, his thick black eyebrows look fake.

'Of course I regard you highly. I asked my secretary to send you a VIP invitation to the Golden Anniversary Dream celebration, but you didn't turn up. As a Party member and confirmed atheist, I have always been wary of the supernatural. But ... experience changes people.' Director Ma is pleased to discover that he hasn't lost his talent for coining wise maxims.

'They say you're a bit of a womaniser, Old Ma. Is that what's got you in trouble? Here, have some tea – it's Iron Goddess of Mercy, grown especially for top government leaders.' Master Wang appears to consider this job beneath him. He fingers his rosary beads for a few seconds, then his thick eyebrows dart up, his eyes sparkle and he pronounces his diagnosis: 'Your vital essence has been dissipated and your original spirit ruptured. There is an intruder in your soul. Calamity is inevitable.'

Director Ma can see that Master Wang is an unusual character, so decides to get straight to the point. 'I need some of Old Lady Dream's Broth of Amnesia,' he says, looking intently into his eyes. 'I've heard you own the secret recipe.'

'No, I don't. If anyone needs it, I have to travel to the netherworld, cross the Yellow Springs and have a private chat with Old Lady Dream. She's a fickle deity though, and doesn't always oblige. More people than hairs on an ox's back have begged me to give them the recipe, desperate to forget their past. But my journeys to the netherworld are not easy, you know. I put my life in mortal danger.' Master Wang's mouth curves into a cynical smile.

'Of course, I understand. If you want help from the deities, you must reward them generously. I will pay whatever it costs, I promise.' Suddenly Yao Jian's square face, slashed at the cheek, flashes before his eyes. *After his warm blood spurted onto my cheeks, he leaned over and spluttered: 'Long live Chairman Mao', before finally choking to death.* Beads of sweat begin to seep from Director Ma's bald scalp.

'Old Lady Dream is even more powerful than you, Mr China Dream! One bowl of her broth, and you'll forget everything – the greatest thinkers, most famous bloggers, your dearest companions. You'll even forget who you are. It's a shame she only serves her broth to the dead, otherwise your China Dream Bureau could sell it to the world, then every country on the planet would embrace the China Dream and obey the orders of the Chinese Communist Party! Ha!' Master Wang cackles loudly and rests his cup of tea on a side table.

'All I want is to delete my past and get back to my job,' Ma Daode says with a shrug. 'I don't care about the China Dream or the Global Dream any more.'

'But if life becomes disconnected from the past, it loses all meaning: "History is the chicken soup of the soul", after all.' Master Wang gives Director Ma a knowing wink. He clearly wants to ingratiate himself with this disgraced leader and con him out of as much money as he can.

'But that's the title of one of my books!' Ma Daode says, his eyes popping in disbelief. 'Don't tell me you bought a copy!'

'How could I *not* buy the book of a top official like you? Look, here it is. Would you do me the honour of signing it?' Before Director Ma's arrival, Master Wang had made sure to place the book close to hand. 'Now tell me, from what age do you want to forget?'

'From the age of fifteen, when I joined the Red Guards.

No, from the age of sixteen, when I joined the violent struggle. Wait – my parents died that year, so I'd like to keep my last memories of them, if possible?' The thought of permanently losing a memory of his parents suddenly makes Ma Daode feel faint.

'You think nothing of deleting other people's dreams and memories. I've heard you've even considered deleting mine. But when it comes to erasing your own, you hesitate! So, tell me, how old were your parents when they passed away?' Master Wang is still wearing his pyjamas and slippers. He doesn't like visitors to stay too long.

'They committed suicide together on 8 February 1968. My father Ma Lei was forty-six and my mother Zhu Mei was forty-five. I suppose I really should erase that terrible night from my mind.' As he utters these words, he feels a sharp pain in his fingers and sees the cheap plywood coffin in which he buried his parents. His hands got so cold that night when he dug the grave that his fingers ached for days afterwards.

'Well, if you want to forget that night, you'll have to wipe out the entire Cultural Revolution, I'm afraid,' says Master Wang, closing his eyes meditatively.

'All right, then. And there are a few episodes from this year I'd like to forget as well.' Ma Daode feels his shirt collar sticking to his neck.

'Girlfriend trouble?' Master Wang asks, wiggling his bare toes. 'That's easy to sort out. I'll just invite your mistresses here and write a spell that will remove you from their minds for ever.'

'What a relief that would be!' Director Ma throws his head right back and stares up at the ceiling, mouth ajar, just the way he does in the evenings after he has drunk too much. His mistress Li Wei loves it when he sits like that: she thinks it makes him look sad and lost. After he slept with her for the first time, he wrote her a solemn promise, swearing on the flag of the Chinese Communist Party that the following year he would divorce his wife and marry her. But he knows that ten years later, she is still waiting for him to honour the pledge.

Director Ma's phone vibrates again. He presses it to his ear and hears a voice whisper: 'Would you like another service from me, Director Ma?' He immediately hangs up. 'I don't believe it!' he says to Master Wang. 'That was a call I got ten years ago, when I was lying in a Shenzhen hotel room after a long conference. I really am being haunted by the spirits of the dead!' He feels as though a pair of hands is tightening around his throat.

'Men and ghosts are intricately entwined. That woman on the phone died two days ago. She just wanted to pay you a visit.' Master Wang falls into silent reverie and slowly passes the beads of his rosary through his fingers. 'Come back here tomorrow evening,' he says at last. 'I will go to the Bridge of Helplessness and get the recipe from Old Lady Dream. As soon as she hands it to me, it will appear to you on a piece of spirit paper that will vanish the moment you read it.'

'I can't thank you enough,' Director Ma says, nodding appreciatively. He feels ghostly fingers smothering his face now, and his tongue grow stiff and numb.

After another visit to Master Wang's house the following evening, Ma Daode walks home, reciting Old Lady Dream's recipe into his phone for the third time. Once he's back in his apartment, he transcribes the three recordings, deletes any repetitions and comes up with what he hopes to be the correct recipe:

1 DROP MOTHER'S MENSTRUAL BLOOD

2 DROPS FATHER'S TEARS

1 BITTER GOURD

1 TEASPOON RICE VINEGAR

1 PINCH SEA SALT

2 DATES

1 DASH YIN ESSENCE

1 DASH YANG ESSENCE

2 GHOST SOULS

METHOD:

WHEN THE MOON REACHES ITS APEX IN THE NIGHT SKY, TURN OFF THE LIGHTS, EMPTY THE INGREDIENTS INTO A PAN AND SIMMER GENTLY UNTIL THE FIFTH WATCH. IMBIBE IN THE MORNING FOR THREE CONSECUTIVE DAYS.

The original recipe appeared to him on a thin piece of paper the size of a playing card. Ma Daode was not able to decipher the netherworld script, so Master Wang read it out to him, and as soon as he came to the end, the paper disappeared in a ball of blue flames.

Ma Daode scratches his head. *Were there not two chillies as well?* He replays the first recording, then the second. It is only on the third that chillies are mentioned, but for some reason the voice he hears belongs not to him but to his father. Ma Daode knows it will be difficult to source all the ingredients. *Perhaps I can replace my mother's menstrual blood with my wife's? No – she has already gone through the menopause. And my father's tears? Maybe I can use my own instead. But where can I find ghost souls, and how could I add them to the soup? This will be more difficult than developing a microchip that can upload the China Dream into the human brain.*

Daunted by the task, Ma Daode takes two swigs from a bottle of vintage Xijiu and listens to the fridge huffing noisily like a runner panting for breath. *It's almost nine o'clock. Why is Juan not back from her fan dancing yet?* He peeps into the sitting room to see if she's there, then goes to his office. Since he filled it with bookshelves, he has rarely ventured inside. He ordered the books online, put them straight on the shelves and hasn't taken one down since. *'One key opens a thousand locks. Armed with Mao Zedong Thought, I will grip my gun for eternity ...'* Ma Daode tries to stop himself singing out loud the song playing in his mind. He is fed up of his adolescent self intruding on his thoughts. It has caused him the loss of his chauffeur-driven car and the suspension from his job. *If I don't destroy my past self, I will lose everything.*

He takes out his phone, dials a number and says: 'Sorry to be calling you so late, Master Wang, it's just I've studied the recipe again. From what I can tell, the soup is a harmonious combination of sweet, sour, hot and bitter. When it is imbibed, all the joys and sorrows of life will flood into the body with such force that every trace of the past will be flushed out. Am I right? My mother's menstrual blood would help keep memories of familial love, I presume, and my father's tears would remind me what gender I am. But my parents are dead, so how will I find those ingredients? And as for the two ghost souls – where on earth can I get hold of those? Without them, though, I'm afraid the soup will be no

131

better than a medicinal potion, with no power to help me start my life anew. Have I understood everything correctly? And what can I use instead of my parents' blood and tears?'

Although annoyed to be disturbed so late at night, Master Wang replies patiently: 'You've examined the recipe in great depth, Director Ma, and have grasped the essentials. I cannot change Old Lady Dream's recipe, I'm afraid, but feel free to make some tweaks of your own. Why not use your parents' ashes instead of their blood and tears?'

'Great idea! Yes – I'll try that,' says Ma Daode, his heart beating faster. 'And the ghost souls?'

'Yes, those will be harder to find. Gathering ghost souls can be deadly dangerous. I tell you what, I'll give you a recipe another client used and you can adjust the proportions to suit your needs. I must go now. We'll talk later.' At this, Master Wang hangs up.

Ma Daode flies into a rage. *Who do you think you are?* he mutters internally with a cold sneer. *One word from me, and you'll rot in jail for the rest of your life. What kind of Master are you, anyway, if you don't know where to find a ghost soul? And if I knew where my parents' ashes were, I wouldn't have come to you in the first place. You want more money? Fine. Here's another 100,000 yuan. Let's see if you refuse to help me now!* He remembers a few years ago paying some men to dig up the ground near the ancient willow tree. They unearthed many bones, but didn't find a pair of skeletons lying side by side. He told the men to look out for a red plastic cover, as his sister had placed their parents' copy of the *Little Red Book* on the plywood coffin before shovelling the earth on top. In the end, they found two skeletons quite close to each other beside the red plastic cover of *Selected Works of Mao Zedong*, but when Ma Daode saw the long hair attached to the female skull and the Red Guard military belt looped around the male spine, he knew that they were not his parents. He paid the men 10,000 yuan each and told them to return the bones to their grave.

How many battles did I fight in? Why wasn't I shot and buried like all those other kids? I remember the day we tried to rescue a rebel faction that had been surrounded in the air-compressor plant – the one below Wolf Tooth Mountain that is now a retirement home for corrupt officials. The Million Bold Warriors had set up two heavy machine guns on a concrete water tank. Our only weapons were staves and rods. Within minutes, the valley was filled with corpses and the piercing cries of the wounded. A boy called Sun Liang who was running by my side got hit in the chest. He reached for my hand, shuddered, then dropped down dead.

Ma Daode opens a drawer and takes out a print of

the family photograph his sister emailed to him. Through the magnifying glass he can see that his mother is smiling, although he can't remember her ever smiling in real life. Her eyebrows look strange as well. He remembers them being arched like his father's, but in this photograph they are straight. Her curly hair is just how he remembers it, though. She often had her hair in rollers when she made rice congee for breakfast, and would take them out and leave them on the windowsill before she went off to work. *Father's face looks as broad as I remember it. What a pity he shaved that morning – he looks like me when I was County Propaganda Chief. And that fountain pen clipped to his shirt pocket – I remember him saying he stole it from a British prisoner-of-war in Korea. It broke after a couple of years, but he still liked to keep it on his pocket. My sister is standing next to my mother. On our way to the photographer's studio, I stepped in a puddle and splashed water onto her skirt. The photographer wiped it off and put a potted plant in front of us to hide our muddy shoes.*

Ma Daode shakes his head. *How tall were my parents? How long would their skeletons be? If I set up a China Dream Research Centre in Garden Square, I'd be able to dig up the ground and search for their bones again.* He stares into his father's eyes and says: 'I remember the milk ice lolly you bought me once when we were waiting

134

for a bus. How delicious it was!' Then he looks at his mother more closely through the magnifying glass and sees the wrinkle running from her mouth to her chin, the two small dots of her nostrils and even the faint creases of her upper eyelids. The comment he hated most as a child was: 'Your eyes are just like your mother's.' But as he looks at her now, face to face, he is happy that they share a resemblance. 'I am your son,' he tells her. 'I wish you hadn't left this world so soon. I miss you. When my hands were cold you used to press them against your stomach to warm them up ...'

A tear falls from his eye and lands on her face. She reaches up from the photograph, strokes his cheek and says: 'What a good son you are. Don't worry, it won't be hard to find us. I'll put out a bone to mark the spot. Just dig into the earth beneath and pull us out. And ask your sister to bring us two pairs of socks. They're inside the chest you sit on at mealtimes. Our feet get so cold at night.'

'Of course, I will do as you ask,' he replies. 'I don't want to forget you or Father. I just want to erase all the crimes I committed and the atrocities I witnessed. It made me so sad the other day to see all those people celebrating their parents' Golden Wedding Anniversary.'

'Your father doesn't blame you. He knows you were just—'

Ma Daode's phone vibrates. It's a message from Master Wang: 1 SLICE GINGER, SUCKED BY A CORPSE; 9 TEASPOONS BLOOD FROM 9 BLACK CATS; 8 TEARS FROM YOUR OWN EYES; 14 DROPS YELLOW SPRING WATER; 1 SPRIG GREEN CORAL; 1 WOLF HEART ... Before he reaches the end, Director Ma glances up and sees that his mother has returned to the photograph. *She wants her old socks? How could she think we'd keep those filthy rags? Still, I wish I didn't have to lose my last memories of her. If only I could get rid of selected episodes. The first one I'd delete would be my fight with Yao Jian. Actually, that fight wasn't just between me and him. A factory worker joined in too. When he raised his hoe to strike me, I shouted: 'Long Live Chairman Mao', assuming I was about to die, but he lost his balance and fell at my feet. I also want to erase the time I told my classmates that my father owned an English fountain pen, and we hauled him up in front of a crowd and I yelled at him: 'Confess your crimes to Chairman Mao!' Yes, those dreadful memories must go ... This new recipe Master Wang has texted me – I'll need to travel to the netherworld to fetch Yellow Spring water, but the rest of the ingredients should be easy to find.*

Ma Daode opens the search engine on his phone and types BLACK CAT. He learns that the American writer, Edgar Allan Poe, wrote a short story called 'The Black

Cat', and that ACCORDING TO CHINESE MYTHOLOGY, BLACK CATS WARD OFF EVIL. KEEP A BLACK CAT BY YOUR FRONT DOOR, AND YOU, YOUR SONS AND GRANDSONS WILL NEVER COME TO HARM. *So black cats banish evil spirits? With nine drops of their blood, I'll be able to fetch water from the netherworld without coming to harm. I must buy nine black cats immediately.*

But after scrutinising the revised recipe again, he decides the female 'yin' elements are too strong, so he deletes the cat blood and replaces the green coral with red. *That should do it.* Now all he needs is water from the Yellow Springs. He leans back in his leather chair, gazes at the photograph on his desk and wonders what would happen if, after drinking his Old Lady Dream's Broth, he forgets who he is. He looks at himself in the photograph, standing in front of his mother in a white vest and shorts, and feels a tide of love wash over him. *I'll bore wells into the ground to extract Yellow Spring water, like companies that drill for oil. Then I'll set up a China Dream Pharmaceutical Plant to manufacture Old Lady Dream's Broth, and my name will go down in history. I'll serve the first batch to a volunteer and see what happens, then others can decide how much to drink, depending on how much they want to forget. I'll make Yuyu drink the first bowl. She's plotting my downfall, I'm sure.*

Director Ma pulls out his *Fragrant Beauties Register* in which he has written all the names of the women he has slept with, and begins to draw up a list of guinea pigs for his Old Lady Dream's Broth. But the names on the page become obscured suddenly by an image of Pan Hua standing in a street of Ziyang, silhouetted against a big character poster ... *No, she wasn't standing outside. It was raining that day, so all the posters had been washed off and were soaking in puddles on the pavements. Only in the Drum Tower stairwell were posters still stuck to the walls. Yes, it was inside the Tower that I saw her silhouette. Her gaze swept down my body like a bolt of lightning, arousing me so deeply I couldn't move.*

When Ma Daode arrived in Yaobang Village as a sent-down youth, he was afraid to visit the wild grove in case he was accused of not drawing a clear line between himself and his Rightist parents. It was not until a year later, when the military took control and quelled the violent struggle for good, that he and his sister went to look for their grave. But by then so many other graves had been dug there, it was impossible to locate it. In 1976, after Mao had died and the Cultural Revolution came to an end, many families returned to the wild grove, unearthed their relatives' skeletons, cremated them and took the ashes home. That was when Pan Hua's bones were removed. In the 1990s, the government imposed a

138

ban on ground burials, and the grove was used again as a secret cemetery by families wanting to avoid the cost of mandatory state cremations. When the Yaobang Industrial Park was being built in 2006, Ma Daode often visited the construction site with the Hong Kong investors, and was always conscious that he was treading on his parents' lost bones.

The line of a song suddenly enters his mind: *'The Party is as dear to me as my own mother. My mother gave birth to my body, but the Party's glory lights up my heart.' Sometimes the fragments from the past that return to my mind are trivial and mundane. But this song holds a special significance to Juan and me. During the first few months in Yaobang, I often heard her sing: 'The Party's glory lights up my heart.' Then one night, I turned off the lights and whispered in her ear: 'I am the Party, so watch my glory light up your heart,' and then we kissed and she screeched with joy.*

That bloody Golden Anniversary Dream! Remembering how he disgraced himself on the podium that day with his deranged ramblings, he slams his cup of tea onto the side table, smashing it to pieces that scatter over the crate of books below. He remembers smashing a bowl in the same way, many years ago, when he glared angrily at his father and shouted: 'All you do every day is write, write, write! You've been denounced for it countless times, but you still won't stop. And because of your stupid stubbornness, I've been kicked out of the Red Guards!'

Director Ma flicks through the notebooks he has filled with records of his illicit affairs. There is a book for each year up until he bought his first mobile phone. He finds a copy of the contract he drew up with Yuyu, in which he confessed to their relationship and pledged to pay her 100,000 yuan for her lost virginity, which she would use to fund her studies abroad. Last month, she resigned from her job and had an abortion, as agreed in the contract. Director Ma stares wistfully at their red thumbprints that lie nestled together at the bottom of the page like two tiny Easter eggs.

Why is this young generation never satisfied? Only people of my age, who grew up with nothing, know how to be content with their lot. I remember on the way to the village school one morning, when my family was living in Yaobang during the Great Famine, I tricked the little girl called Tianmu into giving me her last baked goose dropping. I wanted to save it for my mother, but on my way home that afternoon, I was so starving I ate it myself. It tasted like dried fish. I'd wanted my mother to try it, because she had told me that before she married she had worked for an English family and had acquired a taste for pungent-smelling Western food. Sometimes, when she was making new soles for our shoes, she'd bring out old

magazines to use for the patterns, and we'd glimpse photo-
graphs of foreign gardens and fountains and blonde
women in floral dresses. She told us she had once knitted
a jumper for young Henry. After the Red Guards discov-
ered she had worked for a foreign family, they dragged
her to a struggle meeting and thrashed her face with a
leather shoe. When she came home, her cheeks were red
and swollen and the corner of her mouth was bleeding.
She had always looked youthful and elegant, dressing in
well-fitting clothes, her black hair pinned back with white
clips. But after that night, she suddenly looked old.
IF I CAN'T SEE YOU, MY EYES WILL LOSE THEIR SPARK.
IF I CAN'T HOLD YOU, MY HANDS WILL LOSE THEIR
WARMTH. I'VE PAID THE 10,000 YUAN DEPOSIT. PLEASE
SEND ME ANOTHER 150,000 YUAN TOMORROW, OR THE
DEAL WILL FALL THROUGH. This text from Number 8,
the hostess from the Red Guard Nightclub, flatters and
then angers Ma Daode. *That fake Pan Hua! First she asks*
me to pay for nose and genital piercings. Now she wants
me to buy her the beauty salon below her apartment.
Money – that's all these young women care about!

His wife Juan arrives home at last and says: 'So you're
a social media star now, apparently! Auntie Shu's
daughter follows you on Weibo, and would like a signed
copy of your book.' Auntie Shu walks up behind her,
catching her breath. She's wearing red, high-heeled shoes

and a flamenco dress and is holding a large silk fan. 'Yes, my daughter's a huge admirer of yours, Director Ma,' she says. 'You're a celebrated author!'

'No, not at all – I'm just an ordinary cultural official,' Director Ma replies, closing his drawer. Aunty Shu's daughter is a dowdy girl who works in the Drum Tower ticket office. He takes a copy of *Cautionary Sayings for the Modern World* from the crate below him, turns to the title page and writes: BE KIND TO YOURSELF AND YOUR HAPPINESS WILL BE UNPARALLELED. As he scribbles his signature, he hears his wife gently kick the pieces of broken cup from under the bookshelves, out of sight.

The dream of the red tower

On his second day back in the office following his two-week suspension, Director Ma unscrews the flask of Old Lady Dream's Broth that he prepared as well as he could the night before, takes a large swig, then flings open his window and yells that he wants to fly to Garden Square. Hu grabs him by the belt, tells him to consider the political consequences of such unhinged behaviour, and pushes him back down onto the swivel chair.

Three guards swiftly appear and escort him from the China Dream Bureau to the security department on the ground floor. The peculiar stench of his Old Lady Dream's Broth drifts through the White House and the Gate of Heavenly Peace and lingers in the air for days. After this unfortunate episode, Ma Daode is diagnosed with manic depression and schizophrenia, and is banned from returning to his office. But he insists he is perfectly fine, and that his temporary loss of sanity was caused by incorrect proportions of ingredients in the broth's recipe. He vows to find the correct formula through repeated trials, then apply for a patent, return to the China Dream Bureau and market the potion throughout the world under the brand name China Dream Soup.

In today's trial, he pours a cup of blood from a black cat into an empty Coca-Cola bottle, then adds a wolf's heart, a slice of ginger that has been soaked for a week inside a corpse's mouth, and a few drops of the foul-smelling Yellow Spring water he bought from Master Wang for 100,000 yuan. After a good shake, he dips his tongue into the acrid concoction. The taste seems fine to him. All he needs to do now is go to the wild grove, shed a few tears and add them to the bottle; then he can swallow the contents and see what he forgets. He decides to set off at once, but as soon as he steps outside onto the main road, yesterday vanishes from his mind. Terrified he might forget who he is as well, he rushes back inside, writes: MA DAODE, DIRECTOR OF CHINA DREAM BUREAU, on the lid of a shoebox and ties it around his neck with a shoelace. Then he goes back out and sets off again.

The cold October wind fills him with a solitary gloom. He tries to retrieve some memories from this morning. *I put on my suit and checked myself in the mirror as I adjusted my tie. It's blood red. One of my shoes is black;*

the other is one of the two-toned brogues that belonged to my father. He looks down at his feet. *Yes, there it is. Then there was Juan barefoot in the kitchen, sleepily stretching her arms, reminding me to take my medication. Who does she think she is? I won't touch those bloody pills! Then the phone rang. Was it my daughter? No. Was it that girl, Yuyu, who's gone to Birmingham University? No – she phoned a few days ago, threatening to come back next year unless I send her more money. Nasty piece of work! Still, she's not as bad as the estate agent Wendi who reported me to the Political and Legal Affairs Commission. None of that matters any more, though. When my China Dream Soup is in the shops, all those people who mocked me for failing to produce the China Dream Device will have to watch me return to the China Dream Bureau in a blaze of glory.*

He walks on with a determined frown. Now that his arse has enlarged in old age, he feels steadier on his feet. All he can see of the people in the distance is a swathe of unblinking black eyes advancing towards him like a sheet of rain. This road that runs from Revolution Boulevard to Drum Tower Street used to be a cobbled lane lined with stalls where farmers from outlying villages would sell their produce, but since Ziyang was promoted from county to municipal status, it has been expanded into a busy four-lane road that connects with the provincial highway. Ma Daode has never walked along it before, as his journey to work follows a more northerly route. But today he wants to go to the wild grove on the other side of Magpie Bridge, and this is the shortest way. He notices a few dilapidated apartment buildings stranded along the new road, their balconies still festooned with colourful laundry, gleaming in the sun. Bearing right into the newly pedestrianised Drum Tower Street, he sees that English-style street lamps have been erected along the pavements all the way to the refurbished Drum Tower at the end. He looks at the hazy mist hovering over the sparkling new paving stones, and remembers how the cobbled streets that used to run through this old district were always encrusted with dirt. This is where Ma Daode grew up. It was along this street that he and his wife Juan used to take their evening strolls. Feeling an itch at the back of his throat, he breaks into a military song: "'Forward! Forward! We soldiers face the sun, our feet stamping the earth of the Motherland ...'" It is about ten in the morning now. People are sitting at street-side tables eating corn gruel; shopkeepers are unloading crates of instant noodles and stacking them up outside their shops. A farmer sitting at a nearby table shouts out as he passes: 'Bit early in the morning to be out promoting the China Dream, isn't it, Director Ma?'

Ma Daode looks at this farmer's buck teeth and says: 'Hey, you're Gao Wenshe, aren't you, the mushroom

146

grower from Yaobang Village? You remind me so much of your sister.'

'I don't have a sister, and there's no Yaobang Village either.' A grain of yellow corn is stuck at the corner of his mouth, and his hair is still flattened where he slept on it.

'You did have a sister,' Ma Daode replies, 'but during the Great Famine, your mother was so hungry, she had no choice but to kill her and eat her.' Ma Daode feels a surge of compassion as this long-buried memory returns to him.

'Just bugger off, will you! I don't have a mother or a sister, and you and your corrupt officials demolished Yaobang Village months ago to line your filthy pockets!'

'You did have a sister. Her name was Gao Tianmu. I swear on Chairman Mao.' Ma Daode wants to make the gesture of an oath but can't remember where to place his right hand.

'Fuck you and fuck your China Dream!' Gao Wenshe shouts. Then he jumps up from his seat, rips the sign off Ma Daode's neck and flings it onto the pavement.

'Ungrateful bastard! If it hadn't been for your sister you wouldn't be alive now. Your mother had to eat her after you were born so that she could produce enough milk for you.' Ma Daode picks up the sign from the ground and continues towards the Drum Tower.

Although he has taken a few sips of the China Dream Soup, not all of his childhood memories have been wiped out. Gao Tianmu's little face, as pale as candlewax, is still etched in his mind. He remembers the morning when, on their way to the village school, she was so hungry she had to keep stopping to rest, but he still managed to trick her into giving him the baked goose dropping she was clutching in her hand. As her family had run out of food, her mother had resorted to stealing goose droppings from their neighbour's yard and baking them in the wok to save the family from starvation.

An elderly woman appears in front of him. He recognises her as the old woman who spoke at the Golden Anniversary Dream celebration. 'You're the mother of Pan Hua, aren't you? How sprightly you look today. Have you come out to buy some regional snacks?' Ma Daode feels wide awake now, and decides that his China Dream Soup gives an even better boost to the brain than coffee.

'Sprightly? What do you mean? I'm stone cold dead,' she says, looking deep into his eyes.

'So you've drunk Old Lady Dream's Broth of Amnesia then?' he asks. 'Have you crossed the Bridge of Helplessness yet? You do remember me, don't you? I'm Director Ma.'

'Every dead soul must drink a cup of Old Lady Dream's

Broth before they cross the Bridge of Helplessness and return to the mortal world. But when I reached the bridge, Old Lady Dream wasn't there. An old school friend was ladling it out instead, and he let me cross without drinking any. That's why I can still remember my past life. I've returned to the World of the Living to search for my daughter's reincarnation.'

Ma Daode wonders whether hostess Number 8 from the Cultural Revolution Nightclub might be the reincarnation of Pan Hua after all. 'Do you think she is here in Ziyang?' he asks.

'She won't have gone far. I've worked out she'd be forty by now. I know I will find her.' The old woman sounds determined.

'See this concoction here?' he says. 'I call it China Dream Soup. It's a refined version of Old Lady Dream's recipe. Please try some.'

She gives the bottle a sniff and returns it to him. 'No, thank you. It smells much more pungent than Old Lady Dream's Broth.'

'When I reach the wild grove, I will add some of my tears to it and swallow it in one gulp, and your daughter will vanish from my mind for ever.' Ma Daode feels a strong connection to this woman, and wants to prolong the conversation.

'I can see from your eyes that you have a debt of

blood,' she says. 'You won't be allowed across the Bridge of Helplessness. You'll be flung into the River of Forgetting and will spend eternity as a feral ghost.' Then she turns and walks away.

A feral ghost? Ma Daode can't believe his ears. *What an injustice! I only fought in those battles to defend Mao Zedong Thought. How can I be punished for that? When our East is Red faction and a unit of rebel workers reached the railway station, hoping to make our escape, we discovered that the Million Bold Warriors were already standing on the roof of our train behind two large machine guns. Wives and children of the rebel workers were waiting for us, huddled in a corner. As soon as they saw us, they rushed onto the platform, and were instantly gunned down. Children caught in the crossfire stood gripping pillars, frozen with fear. No one came to take the corpses away. They lay there for days, growing purple and swollen like rotten aubergines. I want to scrub out all those dreadful scenes. But what I want to forget the most is my shameful betrayal of my father. When I see him again, I will fall to my knees and beg for his forgiveness.*

Hearing a message buzz on his phone, Ma Daode wishes he could send a text to his father, although he knows full well there are no relatives in his list of contacts. Since his parents died, he and his sister have not even spent one Chinese New Year together. *My sister put their copy of* Selected Works of Mao Zedong *safely in her bag, then gathered together the other belongings the Red Guards hadn't burned, and set fire to them in the back yard. The letter my mother left for us was written in green ink. Her delicate handwriting sloped to the right, while my father's sloped to the left. A few months after their burial, my sister moved far away to Xinjiang Province.*

HOW I WISH I WERE YOUR MOBILE PHONE: HELD CLOSE TO YOUR CHEST, GAZED UPON BY YOUR EYES, CHERISHED IN YOUR HEART. *Who sent this one?* Ma Daode wonders. *Was it that woman who chose the music for my China Dream promotional video?* As soon as he deletes her text, she evaporates from his mind.

On his right, he sees the newly built Rich Family Supermarket. The stone lions flanking the front gates and the horizontal tablet above the entrance give the modern building an air of antiquity. This is where Ma Daode's family home once stood. He came here last month after it was demolished and the supermarket was being built. He notices that a Qingfeng Dumpling Store has been opened on the ground floor. *I used to sleep in a room just where that dumpling store is now, on a cast-iron bed facing south. Our home was a two-storey grey-brick house. The front door and window casements were painted dark red. When my father came home from work, he would sit on a stool in the front yard and read his newspaper, and would only come*

151

inside when the lights were turned on and mosquitoes began to swarm around him. The house was damp and the windows were too high up. When the front door was closed, we couldn't see a thing. Only when my mother was putting water on the stove to boil and calling out to my father would the living room feel a little cosier. After my father changed from being County Chief of Ziyang to a condemned Rightist, the house was divided and shared with two other families. My parents built an attic room in our portion of the house for my sister and me to sleep in. We loved our new smaller home in which the four of us would shuffle about, continually bumping into each other. The LONG LIVE MARXISM-LENINISM slogan I painted on our living-room wall is now daubed over the dumpling store's front window. Or are my eyes deceiving me? When the Red Guards stormed into our home, they ordered my parents to stand facing the wall, heads bowed. The hand-sewn cloth shoes on my parents' feet looked out of place in that atmosphere of terror.

I ran about, showing my fellow Red Guards where our family's bourgeois belongings were hidden. Song Bin, dressed in khaki fatigues and a red armband, dragged my mother's leather suitcase down from the attic and kicked it open, and out poured relics from the old society: a silk cheongsam, a pair of high-heeled shoes, a necklace, a bracelet and a gold-embroidered leather handbag. The enraged Red Guards hurled these incriminating objects at

*my mother and shouted: 'Destroy old thoughts, old culture,
old habits, old customs! Destroy the Four Olds and establish the Four News! Eliminate reactionary ideology!' But
then they kicked open the other leather suitcase, pulled
out an old family album, and from between its pages fell
a faded photograph of my mother with the English family
she had worked for.*

*A second later I heard them howl: 'Down with the female
spy, Zhu Mei,' and my mind exploded. I knew I was
doomed. In a manic rage, they ransacked our home, flung
everything they could into a heap outside and set light to
it. To prove my commitment to the revolution, I picked
through burning pesticide bottles, paraffin lamps, mirrors
and shoehorns, and pulled out from the flames a mimeo-
graphed pamphlet on the policies of Chairman Mao and
the first newsletter from Red Sun Secondary School which
Song Bin had given me, put them carefully into my bag
and walked away under the contemptuous gaze of my
classmates and neighbours. Being the son of a Rightist was
bad enough, but being the son of an agent of Western
imperialists was unforgivable.*

*I was expelled from the Red Guards the following
morning. But I didn't lose heart. Instead, I resolved to
learn the* Quotes of Karl Marx *off by heart and throw
myself into the revolution with greater zeal. When East
is Red took me under their wing, I cut all ties with my*

family and devoted my entire being to Chairman Mao. Although I did occasionally sneak home for some food and a good night's sleep, I never uttered another word to my parents, not even on the last evening we spent together just before they killed themselves.

Passers-by begin to surround Ma Daode and point at him. 'Is he on his way to petition the China Dream Bureau?' one man asks. The supermarket security guard standing by a stone lion says: 'If you want to buy something, go inside – don't just stand here blocking the entrance.'

Ma Daode points at the ancient stone tablet above the door, and shouts: 'Tear down that feudal artefact at once! Eliminate old ideologies and old customs of the exploiting class!' Feeling unsettled, he looks down at the sign he is holding that tells him he is Ma Daode, Director of the China Dream Bureau. *But which Ma Daode am I?* After a brief hesitation, he hangs the sign around his neck again.

Song Bin walks out of the dumpling store and says: 'Coming to "mingle incognito with the masses", are you, old friend? Wonderful! Step inside and try some of our President Xi dumplings.'

Director Ma has no choice but to shake Song Bin's hand. 'Your wife's very clever to have opened a branch here, just as the China Dream era is kicking off,' he says. 'I hope she makes a success of it.'

'You think Hong opened this place? She hasn't a clue how to run a business! Truth is, with all these officials being had up for corruption and womanising lately, I thought I should take early retirement, just to be on the safe side. So this dumpling store is my little escape route! You've done well, though, Daode. Out of all of us from Red Sun Secondary School, you have climbed the highest. But it can't have been easy. There are so many regulations to comply with these days, aren't there? So much red tape!' Song Bin flashes a knowing smile, and Ma Daode understands at once that he's hoping to wangle a favour. *Devious bastard. Wants me to get some government department off his back, does he? He's always just looking out for himself. In the violent struggle, he avoided most of the bloodiest battles by hiding in the Million Bold Warriors headquarters, making mimeographs of their weekly reports.*

'I did rise high, but it didn't last,' Ma Daode replies. 'Like a live crab immersed in boiling water: as soon as I turned red hot, I was dead.' In his pockets, Ma Daode is clutching his phone with his left hand and the bottle of China Dream Soup with his right. He longs to extricate himself from his former classmate.

'Everyone gets knocked down now and then,' Song Bin continues. 'Think of your father: just because his hairstyle was like Chairman Mao's, Red Guards accused him of

155

plotting to supplant the Great Helmsman. They sheared off all his hair and paraded him through Ziyang. I remember him being marched down this very street. I joined the crowd in shouting: "If Ma Lei doesn't confess his crime, we will destroy him." I should really reflect on those times, when I have a chance. Anyway, it sounds like the China Dream Bureau is making great strides. I hear it's taken control of all the local websites and social media platforms. Seems like Hu is doing a good job of holding the fort in your absence.'

'You ransacked our home, Song Bin,' Ma Daode says, staring straight at his monkey-like face. 'Right here, where we're standing now. You persecuted my mother and father so brutally they took their own lives. Your Million Bold Warriors slaughtered three hundred East is Red members. This road was a river of blood. Have you forgotten everything?'

'But East is Red murdered five hundred of us! And remember: you were the one who told us to search your house. You led us here yourself. I swear on Chairman Mao I never killed one person. Not one.' When Song Bin closes his mouth, his thin lips disappear.

'A thousand people were killed in Ziyang. We both fought in the battles. Don't pretend you have no blood on your hands. The day we attacked the general post office, you stabbed a man called Zhao Yi with a three-pronged spear!' Ma Daode jabs his chest to show where the weapon entered Song Bin's victim. Wanting to bring the conversation to a close, he says: 'Go on, spit it out then! Which department has been on your back? Industry and Commerce, Public Security, Fire Prevention … ?'

'Well, as it happens, it's your China Dream Bureau. Your online administrators have encrypted the dream I had last night. I asked them to let me access it just now, but they refused. They said it's a Cultural Revolution dream.'

'They wouldn't deny you access just because of that,' Ma Daode replies. 'You must have said something to annoy them.'

'Well, I did tell them I'm the same age as President Xi. I said that he and I were both Red Guards in the Cultural Revolution, and were exiled to Yanhe County together …'

'Ah, no wonder! You'll be labelled an "overzealous Red Guard" for that! Roping President Xi into your affairs – what a nerve! If you hadn't worked for the government for so many years, you'd be in serious trouble. What's wrong with you? You've retired already, but you still don't know how to behave!'

I remember the look of hatred on Song Bin's face when he terrorised our teachers. He slapped our maths teacher so hard, it sounded like he was swatting a fly against a

157

concrete wall. Her cheek turned bright purple. Ma Daode looks at the new slogan painted on the supermarket's exterior wall: THE COMMUNIST PARTY IS GOOD, THE PEOPLE ARE HAPPY! and sees, hidden beneath it, an older slogan that says: TO PROTECT CHAIRMAN MAO'S REVOLUTIONARY LINE, FIGHT BLOODY BATTLES TO THE BITTER END!

'Soon every dream about the Cultural Revolution will be eradicated, though,' Ma Daode continues. 'See this bottle of China Dream Soup? If all goes to plan, the nightmares that plague our minds will be swept away and replaced with the brand-new China Dream. You and I will be able to forget past sorrows and forge new futures for ourselves!' He walks away, then glances back and says: 'I gave you a set of Sino-Russian Friendship stamps at school. The twenty-two-cent one had a portrait of Stalin. It must be worth a fortune today.'

Indignant at his refusal to help, Song Bin puts his hands on his hips and shouts: 'What a great memory you have! Come back later and try some Xi dumplings, and we'll have a proper talk.'

Ma Daode sees a tricycle cart parked near the Drum Tower. He goes over to it and says to the owner: 'Chairman Mao commanded us to struggle with words, not weapons. Quick, unload all those dangerous bulbs of garlic from your cart and hand them over to the masses.'

'Think you're an urban-management officer, do you?' the farmer sneers. 'Don't boss me about. If you want some of my garlic, they're twenty-five yuan a crate. They're grown for export to South Korea. A hundred per cent organic. If you don't want any, bugger off.'

'Don't you know who I am? I made that!' Ma Daode points to the China Dream promotional video playing on the giant screen attached to the Drum Tower. Right now, it is showing his mistress, the young entrepreneur called Claire, getting out of bed in a pink nightgown, opening a window and gazing out at a blue sky.

'Shut up, you filthy petitioner – you're a disgrace to the city,' the farmer says to Ma Daode, pushing him away; then he spits his cigarette stub onto the ground and crushes it out with his shoe.

Director Ma feels trapped between his two selves. Whether he speaks through the one to his left or to his right, he can't seem to find the right words. He proceeds to the Drum Tower. The ticket office hasn't opened yet. Without thinking, he heaves himself over the wooden fence, walks through the unlocked door and slowly climbs up the steep wooden stairs.

When he reaches the Drum Tower's lofty balcony, he gazes out over the city. He can see that most of the old town is now a mass of high-rise buildings. The Monument to the Revolution, county hospital and Cultural Palace were demolished years ago. All that remains unchanged is the Fenshui River that flows sluggishly along the old road to the west. *Why did my parents kill themselves?* A gentle breeze blows past, lifting some leaves from the square below. He looks down at the two-toned brogue on his right foot. *Those shoes are the only belongings I inherited from my father. Why am I wearing one of them now? I remember the day Mao's earth-shattering slogan* TO MAKE REVOLUTION IS NO CRIME; TO REBEL IS JUSTIFIED *was painted on the wall of this tower. I took out my notebook and faithfully copied it down. My father was denounced and beaten countless times during the months that followed, but so were millions of other people and they managed not to lose hope. The night I was summoned home, why didn't my parents warn my sister and me that they were planning to kill themselves? Of course, my father never recovered from the heartbreak I inflicted on him when I told the Red Guards to ransack our home ...* Ma Daode feels struck with remorse. He wishes he could walk over to his parents now and put his arms around them.

The phone in his pocket judders. It's a message from his daughter: YOU SHOULD INVITE BRITISH FAMILIES TO CHINA AND SEND CHINESE FAMILIES TO BRITAIN ON BILATERAL CULTURAL EXCHANGES. IT WOULD BE MUCH MORE MEANINGFUL FOR BOTH SIDES THAN RUSHED VISITS TO THE USUAL TOURIST SITES ... She advises him to set up a travel agency and put the idea in motion. Ma Daode wonders whether these exchanges would belong to a China Dream or a British Dream. He notices people on the square looking up at him or perhaps at the huge screen below the balcony. When the China Dream Bureau opened bids to erect a giant screen here to broadcast promotional films and public-service announcements, many businesses vied for the deal, offering bribes of cash and beautiful women, but Ma Daode turned them all down and awarded the contract to his oldest lover, Li Wei, who was in fact the most suitable candidate as she was already renting the tower.

'Have you gone up there to kill yourself?' yells an elderly volunteer security guard with a red armband around her left sleeve. 'Come down at once!'

'Look at this!' Ma Daode shouts, climbing onto the balcony's crenellated edge and pointing at the sign hanging from his neck.

A few people huddle together and begin to talk among themselves:

'Bet he's a migrant worker trying to drum up some cash.'

'No – he's probably a peasant petitioning the authorities about the demolition of his house.'

'We should call the police. He's creating a disturbance.'

The garlic seller walks over and says to them: 'No, he's just a madman who thinks he's a government official. Hey, idiot! If you've got the balls, jump!'

Ma Daode clears his throat and launches into a speech: 'Comrades, battle companions, see this sign? It's true: I really am the director of the China Dream Bureau, a municipal government leader. But today, I want to speak to you, not as an official, but as an ordinary Ziyang resident. I was born and bred here. For four years I was banished to Yaobang, over there, to be re-educated by the peasants.' Ma Daode points to the west. 'Now I work on the fifth floor of that huge government and Party headquarters.' He points to the north. 'What is this in my hand, you may wonder?' He raises the Coca-Cola bottle.

The throng below yells: 'It's a petrol bomb! Quick – run!'

'No, come back!' Ma Daode replies. 'It's not a bomb! It's a new, improved version of Old Lady Dream's Broth of Amnesia, which I have named China Dream Soup. In a moment you will discover how it can magically banish your nightmares and replace them with the China Dream. No need for pills or injections, or even the China Dream Device. One sip of this soup and you can make a clean break with the past ...'

'I've seen his toad-like face before,' says a voice in the

crowd. 'He cut the ribbon at the grand opening of Ten Thousand Fortunes Company.'

'Old Lady Dream's Broth?' another man cries out. 'That's only drunk by dead souls who need to forget their past lives before they are reborn into new bodies. I've never heard of a living person drinking it before. Go on then, you fool. Take a sip and see what happens!'

'I will drink it, but before I wipe out all my memories, I want to see my parents one last time,' Ma Daode says, pointing towards Garden Square twelve kilometres away. 'My unfilial behaviour drove them to their grave. But I have changed. I have changed entirely, inside and out, down to the very marrow of my bones.'

'Aren't you the son of Ma Lei and Zhu Mei?' an old man in glasses calls out. 'They were good people, those two. In the Cultural Revolution they were paraded through the streets every day.'

'Yes, it's him! The son of the Rightist. He joined East is Red, and could fight with knives, lances and pistols, as well as his bare fists, and was a master of kung fu. I once saw him run straight towards the barrel of a gun. He was fearless!' The man now speaking is wearing blue overalls and has no head.

Seeing the large number of people who have gathered in the square to gawp, Song Bin brings out crates of steamed dumplings from the Qingfeng Dumpling Store, loads them onto a trolley and then, with his wife, wheels it through the throng shouting: 'Try some Xi dumplings. Pale and plump, soft and tender! Who could resist? Only ten yuan a pair.'

'Officer Ma, I'm Comrade Chun, reporting for duty,' a cross-eyed boy cries out from the crowd. Ma Daode looks down at his old friend, and sees that the two bullets that struck him in the shoulder exited through the waist. It must have been a high-calibre machine gun because there is no blood around the wounds.

'Comrade Chun, when we buried you, I placed two bullets in your hand so that you could avenge your death in the netherworld,' Ma Daode cries back, feeling the burden of his past weigh heavily on his shoulders. He addresses the crowd again: 'See, if you don't drink this China Dream Soup, the past and the present form a tangled web from which it becomes impossible to break free. I'm sure you all have terrible memories you long to get rid of. Well, if you open this bottle of soup, add a few of your own tears, mix it all up and take a sip, your past will vanish as swiftly and permanently as a text you delete from your phone. So, for a life of unbridled joy, drink China Dream Soup!' Ma Daode sees that the square below is now filled with people, but their faces are blank. 'Whoever wants a free taste, raise your hand!' he shouts. A sea of hands rises above the crowd. 'Wonderful. Now,

164

just think of something sad that happened to you in the past and get ready to shed a few tears.'

'That's easy – my wife left me last year to work in a factory in Guangdong, and she refuses to come back,' says a migrant worker squatting on a street corner.

'I've never cried about anything in my life, but my heart is full of sorrow,' says a man with a bald patch. Then he crunches a clove of garlic and bites into a dumpling.

'My newborn son was strangled to death by a family-planning doctor, right in front of me,' says a woman with a blue hairband. 'I wept so much, I have no tears left to cry. What should I do?'

'Borrow someone else's,' suggests Ma Daode. 'Those who have tears, lend them to those who have none. Your reward will come in the next life. Now, let's all travel back in time to the Cultural Revolution and sing together: "Chairman Mao's books are my favourite books. I read them a thousand times, ten thousand times. When I absorb their profound meaning, my heart glows with warm joy ..."'

'Your heart may be glowing with warm joy, you bastard, but mine is fucking stone cold! In fact, let me rip out your heart, then we can see how bloody warm it is!' This boy's bloodied forehead looks like a smashed watermelon. He's wearing dirty overalls and a Million

Bold Warriors armband. Ma Daode recognises him as a boy he kicked off the flat roof of a building. *Yes, I tied his arms back with rope and with one sharp kick sent him flying over the edge. I trudged back home through the snow in his leather boots. The battle continued for days. When I returned a week later, I heard that the Drum Tower had been set alight with petrol bombs. With the help of rebel workers from the Agricultural Machinery Factory and the Red Sword Combat Team, the Million Bold Warriors captured the tower and cut off the escape routes out of the city. Pan Hua was stranded up here on the balcony. After a flaming bottle struck her in the chest, she leapt over the edge and soared to the Yellow Springs, her clothes and hair ablaze.*

'We must put the past behind us, and look ahead, look ahead. That's why I made this soup ...' Ma Daode answers, struggling to find an adequate response to the young man he killed.

'Come down, Ma Daode, and open the door for me!' his mistress Li Wei shouts up to him. 'I need to get into my office.' She is wearing a woollen dress and knee-high leather boots. Her long glossy hair looks as though it has just been blow-dried in a salon.

'Ignore her – she belongs to the Million Bold Warriors!' Ma Daode shouts down sternly.

'Don't pretend not to know me,' Li Wei replies, craning

166

her neck up to look at him. 'I'm Li Wei, your oldest lover. Come down right now. I'm renting this building, and if anything bad happens here, I'll be ruined.' The giant screen casts a blue light over her terrified face.

'But my lover is called Pan Hua. At the height of the violent struggle, she leapt from this tower shouting: "Long live Chairman Mao!"'

'Stop it, Ma Daode!' Li Wei yells, stamping her feet and beginning to sob. 'You are the only man I have been with in my whole life. Stop acting like a madman and come down at once.'

'Don't worry, he won't jump,' says a woman who has just bought some garlic and dumplings. 'He promised to give me a sip of his China Dream Soup so I can forget the misery of my past. I trust him!'

'You're just a little squirt, an East is Red nobody,' cries the boy with the bloodied forehead. 'But I'm the Million Bold Warriors communications officer. If you hadn't kicked me off the roof, I'd be Propaganda Chief of Ziyang by now.'

Ma Daode draws a deep breath of air and savours the delicious scent of pork dumplings and raw garlic. *Just a drop of black vinegar, and the taste would be sublime.*

'I don't care about any of you any more. Once I drink this soup you will all be gone. That other Ma Daode will be gone as well and I will be free at last!' Ma Daode lifts the bottle to his eyes and tries to shed a tear, but realises he will only be able to cry when he sees his parents again.

His secretary, Hu, calls out from below: 'I've kept this to myself all this time, but I must tell you now. During the violent struggle, your East is Red faction staged an exhibition of counter-revolutionary criminals. My mother was one of your exhibits. You locked her in a wooden cage for days and let visitors jab her with bamboo rods and spit in her face.' He points to the ghostly figure with long white hair who is standing beside him.

'I recognise you, old lady!' Ma Daode says. 'You worked in the county supply office. But why are you a ghost? We didn't kill you.' He remembers that she was a lively woman with tightly permed hair. During a street battle waged against her rebel faction, he raised his stick and prepared to strike her on the neck, but his friends gathered round and said: 'Wait, don't kill her. Make her lick a corpse instead.' So he dragged her over to a fallen comrade and forced her to lick the blood from his bludgeoned face.

'I'm here to assist the troops,' says a teenager whose chest is riddled with bullet holes. 'Don't worry – it wasn't you who shot me. We're all desperate to try your soup, so stop talking about it and give us some!'

'Which faction do you belong to?' asks Cross-eyed Chun, walking over to him.

'I'm a Red Guard from the provincial university,' the teenager answers. 'I've been deployed here to support the Million Bold Warriors.'

'Bastard!' Chun shouts, pouncing on top of him. 'Let me avenge my death!' The two youths wrestle to the ground and tear at each other's clothes and hair.

Ma Daode looks down and sees an East is Red unit line up in front of the Drum Tower entrance to prevent a gang of Million Bold Warriors from breaking in. The two groups stand facing each other, hurling insults back and forth. Then he looks over to the square and sees thousands of Red Guards begin to flood in from all sides. Caught in the chaotic scrum of people and ghosts, Li Wei sobs: 'You promised we would never part, Ma Daode! During all these years, my love for you has never waned. Why are my gleaming white thighs and the moist sanctuary between them not enough to keep you by my side?'

'My heart belongs to Pan Hua, but she died many years ago.' Ma Daode gazes out at the impenetrable sea of people and, feeling as though he is performing in a tragic ballet, assumes an expression of pained sorrow.

'I pity poor Juan being married to an unfaithful bastard like you!' shouts Song Bin's wife, Hong. 'May this be the last thing you ever eat!' She snatches a dumpling from the trolley and tries to fling it at Ma Daode, but it hits the China Dream screen instead, its juice spurting out in an oily mist. As Song Bin grasps hold of her hands to stop her throwing any more, Ma Daode shouts down to her: 'You'd be better off keeping an eye on your own husband, Hong! Just check the messages on his phone.' At this, Hong breaks free and punches Song Bin hard in the face, then pursues him through the crowd as he tries to flee.

'But look, I *am* Pan Hua,' Li Wei calls out. 'My soul is reincarnating into Li Wei's body so that I can be with you again. After I fell from that tower and was buried in the wild grove, you were the only classmate who visited my grave. That is why I want to return to you.' As these words leave her mouth, Li Wei transforms into Pan Hua, wearing a faded army uniform and a red scarf around her neck. Only her long glossy hair remains unchanged.

'But remember that pamphlet the Red Guards wrote called "Crimes of Rightist Ma Lei, husband of a female spy who worked for an English family"? You grabbed one from a pile and copied every word of it into your notebook. You despised me.' Ma Daode looks over to the White House and the Gate of Heavenly Peace.

'I only copied it to understand your parents better. When I reached the end, I realised your mother was a good person after all, and I resolved to fall in love with you.' Since Li Wei has transformed into Pan Hua, her voice has become husky and acquired a Sichuan accent.

'Ah, if only I had known!' he says. 'Now I understand why you were so desperate to rent this tower, Li Wei – I mean, Pan Hua. Your mother is looking for you, by the way. I bumped into her on Drum Tower Street just now.'

Ma Daode notices the red Mao badge pinned to her breast begin to swell. His legs tremble so fiercely he almost topples over the edge of the balcony. In the distance, a roar of belligerent yells rings out, and he sees captives, hands raised in surrender, being herded out of the old general post office by a squad of Red Guards; and on a hemp-sack barricade on the street outside, he sees the mad-eyed boy called Tan Dan waving a Mauser pistol in the air, just as he did over forty years ago after he executed the captives on the river pier in Yaobang.

Pan Hua joins the other East is Red recruits who are pushing the enemy faction away from the ticket office. A small group of Million Bold Warriors runs off to the side, scrambles through a hole in the fence and begins to form a human ladder up the Drum Tower. Voices cry out from the jostling hordes: 'Get out of here, you Million Bold Warrior bastards!'

The garlic seller sees his tricycle cart being toppled over and shouts: 'Why aren't the urban-management officers arresting these bloody hooligans?' A group of Red Guards surrounds Song Bin's trolley of bamboo steamers, yelling: 'We Million Bold Warriors are great!

It's you who should bugger off, you East is Red scum!' Then they open the steamers, grab hold of the small, breast-like Xi dumplings and hurl them at the China Dream screen. One hits the corner of Ma Daode's mouth and falls onto his two-toned brogue. In the distance, he sees a People's Liberation Army truck, packed with more Red Guards and rebel workers, advance along Drum Tower Street. A deafening clamour of gongs and drums melds with piercing battle cries. The flat roofs of every surrounding building are now crammed with onlookers. Propaganda Chief Ding is standing among them, waving a burning red flag. From the huge speakers beside the giant screen below, the new China Dream theme song, with lyrics composed by Ma Daode himself, blares out: 'The China Dream is really good, really good, really good ...'

Above the cacophony, Ma Daode yells: 'Comrades-in-arms! With our blood and our lives we have established the glorious new era of the China Dream. Let us bid farewell to the past and sing in unison: "The Cultural Revolution is really good, really ..." Forgive me, I mean: "The China Dream is really good, really good ..."' Just as he is about to sing 'really good' for the third time, Ma Daode sees his father, an English fountain pen clipped to the pocket of his white shirt and a two-toned brogue on his left foot, being dragged by Song Bin out of the Qingfeng Dumpling Store. A stocky little youth, whom Ma Daode instantly recognises as Yao Jian, then yanks his father's head back, chops off a chunk of his hair, looks up and shouts: 'If you don't jump now, Ma Daode, I'll come up and kick you off myself!' Ma Daode stares in amazement at Yao Jian standing there with blood streaming from his mouth, a pair of scissors in his hand and a pool of blood at his feet, looking exactly as he does in the nightmare vision that haunts his days and nights.

His vision suddenly goes black, and blood begins to spurt from his every orifice. He hurriedly raises his bottle to catch some of the crimson drops. Slowly, he feels his body become relaxed and weightless, and his mind imbued with fresh and unswerving resolve. At the top of his voice he yells: 'Long live Father! Long live Mother! Long live the China Dream!' then he gives the bottle a shake and with a grand flourish sprays its contents over the crowd below. When the foul-smelling China Dream Soup lands on their hair, some people cry, some laugh, others cover their noses and flee like a colony of ants escaping a jet of urine.

The soup's morbid stench inundates every street and lane. Ma Daode smiles. Although he hasn't drunk any yet, his memories have already vanished and his mind is completely clear. He raises his gaze from the sea of blood-red flags and looks straight ahead. The crowd is still lobbing the small, pillowy dumplings at him. But when they enter Ma Daode's line of vision, all he sees are soft white clouds bobbing in the clear blue sky. Everything looks clean and pure. He is certain that this heavenly scene unfolding before him is the China Dream of President Xi Jinping. Summoning every remaining ounce of his energy, he discards his vibrating phone and with the grace of a dancer, leaps off the edge of the balcony and soars upward and onward, towards a beautiful and radiant future.

Afterword

In November 2012, two weeks after being crowned
General Secretary of the Chinese Communist Party and
a few months before being appointed President, Xi
Jinping visited the lavishly refurbished National Museum
of China, a vast Stalinist structure on the eastern edge
of Beijing's Tiananmen Square directly opposite the Mao
Mausoleum. With six other black-suited, blank-faced
members of the Politbureau Standing Committee, he
wandered through 'The Road to Rejuvenation', a huge
exhibition that charts China's modern history from the
First Opium War of 1839 to the present day. In room
after room, photographs and artefacts chronicle China's
humiliation at the hands of colonial powers, the foun-
dation of the People's Republic in 1949 and the nation's
subsequent rise under Communist Party rule. But
nowhere in this cavernous exhibition space is there any

mention of the catastrophes inflicted by Chairman Mao and his successors, such as the Great Leap Forward, a reckless campaign to transform China into a Communist utopia, which caused a famine that claimed over twenty million lives; the mass psychosis of the Cultural Revolution that plunged China into a decade of mob violence, chaos and stagnation; and the 1989 massacre of peaceful pro-democracy protestors in the streets around Tiananmen Square. In this museum, and in the bookshops and classrooms outside it, China's post-1949 history is cleansed of darkness and reduced to an anodyne, joyful fairy tale.

At the end of his visit, Xi Jinping announced his 'China Dream of national rejuvenation', promising that continued Communist rule would lead to even greater economic wealth and restore China to its past glory. Since then, this vague and nebulous slogan has formed the bedrock of his administration. Like the despots who preceded him, he has strengthened his grip on power by suppressing information about the hell that Communism has caused and promising a future para-dise. But utopias always lead to dystopias, and dictators invariably become gods who demand daily worship. As I write, China's rubber-stamp parliament has abolished limits on presidential terms, allowing Xi Jinping to remain president for life. The clumsily titled 'Xi Jinping Thought on Socialism with Chinese Characteristics for a New Era' has been enshrined in the constitution. And recently, the education minister pledged that 'Xi Jinping Thought' will go into textbooks, classrooms and 'the brains of students'.

China's tyrants have never limited themselves to controlling people's lives: they have always sought to enter people's brains and remould them from the inside. In fact, it was the Chinese Communists in the 1950s who coined the term 'brainwashing' ('xinao'). The China Dream is another beautiful lie concocted by the state to remove dark memories from Chinese brains and replace them with happy thoughts. Decades of indoctrination, propaganda, violence and untruths have left the Chinese people so numb and confused, they have lost the ability to tell fact from fiction. They have swallowed the lie that the Party leaders are responsible for the country's economic miracle, rather than the vast army of low-paid workers. The rabid consumerism encouraged in the last thirty years and which, along with inflated nationalism, lies at the heart of the China Dream is turning the Chinese into overgrown children who are fed, clothed and entertained, but have no right to remember the past or ask questions.

But a writer's job is to probe the darkness and, above all, to tell the truth. I wrote *China Dream* out of rage against the false utopias that have enslaved and infan-tilised China since 1949, and to reclaim the most brutal period of its recent history – the 'violent struggle' phase of the Cultural Revolution – from a regime that continues to repress it. The book is filled with absurdities, both real and invented. The China Dream Bureaus, Red Guard Nightclubs and mass wedding anniversary ceremonies for octogenarian couples, for example, really do exist in today's China. The China Dream Soup and neural implant are of course products of my imagination. In my effort to express a higher literary truth, my novels have always melded fact with fiction.

Thirty years ago, I wrote my first book, a fictional meditation on Tibet called *Stick Out Your Tongue*. A few weeks after it was published, the government condemned it as 'spiritual pollution' and ordered all copies to be rounded up and destroyed. Since then, every novel I have written has been banned in the mainland. My name is excluded from official lists of Chinese writers and compendiums of Chinese fiction; it can't even be mentioned in the press. And worse still, for the last six years, the government has denied me the right to return. But I continue to 'write, write, write',

178

like the father of *China Dream*'s protagonist. I continue to take refuge in the beauty of the Chinese language and use it to drag memories out from the state-imposed amnesia, to deride and mock China's despots and sympathise with their victims, while remaining conscious that in evil dictatorships, most people are both oppressor and oppressed. Exile is a cruel punishment. But living in the West allows me to see through the fog of lies that shrouds my homeland, and produce the only kind of writing I care about: the full, truthful, untrammelled expression of an author's vision of the world.

And despite everything, I have not surrendered completely to pessimism. I still believe that truth and beauty are transcendental forces that will outlive man-made tyrannies. I hope that perhaps by the time my children reach my age, one or two of my novels might be found in a bookshop in China. More importantly, I hope that the Chinese Communist Party, that has imprisoned the minds and brutalised the bodies of the Chinese people for almost seventy years, and whose growing influence is beginning to corrupt democracies around the world, will be consigned to dusty exhibition rooms of the National Museum. When that day arrives, I hope the Chinese people will be able to confront the nightmares of the past, speak the truth as they see it without fear of reprisal and follow dreams of their own making, their minds and hearts unchained.

Ma Jian
London, March 2018

A note about the cover

When the artist Ai Weiwei was 'disappeared' by the Chinese government in 2011, in a fit of rage I printed hundreds of black-and-white photographs of him with the message 'Free Ai Weiwei' and, with my then five-year-old daughter, scattered them over his sunflower-seed installation in London's Tate Modern, so that the Turbine Hall was covered with his face. Three years ago, my daughter and I met him in person at his exhibition in London's Royal Academy. When my British publisher asked me for ideas about the cover for this book, I immediately thought of the monumental forest of dead trees that stood at the entrance to the exhibition. They reminded me of the gnarled willow under which Ma Daode's parents lie buried. The bare, jagged branches seemed to convey at once the totalitarian mission to suppress the past and the individual's stubborn quest to remember. When I met up again with Ai Weiwei in Berlin where I have been based for the last year, I asked if we could use a photograph of the trees, but he volunteered instead to design the whole cover. The work of art that he has produced is beyond anything that I could have hoped for. In the shattered branches, I see the brutality of autocracy, the splintering of the self and the human soul's yearning for freedom. It encapsulates everything I wanted *China Dream* to say. I am immensely honoured and grateful that he has given the book such a beautiful and powerful image.

MA JIAN was born in Qingdao, China. He is the author of seven novels, a travel memoir, three story collections, and two essay collections. His work has been translated into twenty-six languages. Since the publication of his first book in 1987, all his work has been banned in China. He now lives in exile in London.

FLORA DREW's translations from the Chinese include Ma Jian's *Red Dust*, *The Noodle Maker*, *Stick Out Your Tongue*, *Beijing Coma*, and *The Dark Road*.